ON
ALL
OTHER
NIGHTS

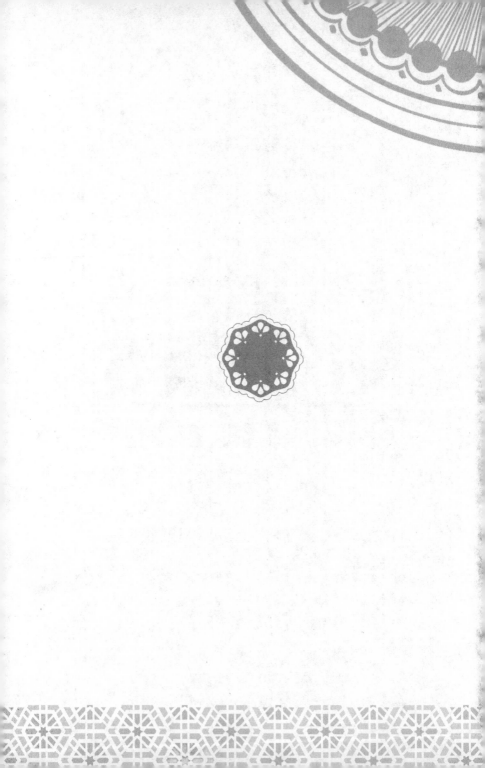

ON ALL OTHER NIGHTS

A PASSOVER CELEBRATION IN 14 STORIES

EDITED BY **CHRIS BARON,**
JOSHUA S. LEVY, AND NAOMI MILLINER

ILLUSTRATED BY **SHANNON HOCHMAN**

AMULET BOOKS • NEW YORK

To you.
If you read these stories, it would be enough.
We hope you write your own, too.

PUBLISHER'S NOTE: This is a work of fiction. Names, characters, places, and incidents are either the product of the author's imagination or used fictitiously, and any resemblance to actual persons, living or dead, business establishments, events, or locales is entirely coincidental.

Cataloging-in-Publication Data has been applied for and may be obtained from the Library of Congress.

ISBN 978-1-4197-6729-6

Text © 2024 respective authors of contributions and other material

General illustrations © 2024 Shannon Hochman

Illustrations for *Double Hallel* © 2024 Amy Ignatow

Book design by Melissa Greenberg and Becky James

Printed and bound in U.S.A.
10 9 8 7 6 5 4 3 2 1

Amulet Books are available at special discounts when purchased in quantity for premiums and promotions as well as fundraising or educational use. Special editions can also be created to specification. For details, contact specialsales@abramsbooks.com or the address below.

Amulet Books® is a registered trademark of Harry N. Abrams, Inc.

ABRAMS The Art of Books
195 Broadway, New York, NY 10007
abramsbooks.com

CONTENTS

Dear Readers,

Welcome to our table.

That's how we see this book—as a table where all are invited. Where we've gathered ourselves, some extraordinary storytellers, and you.

Passover (Pesach, in Hebrew) is a springtime Jewish holiday that commemorates the ancient story of Jews being enslaved in Egypt and ultimately achieving their freedom. A story known as the Exodus.

Like any holiday, there are many traditions, many ways to celebrate. But across the globe, the focus of nearly every Passover is the Seder: a special meal held on the first night (and for many, the first *two* nights) of the weeklong holiday.

The word "Seder" means order, organization, structure. And that's a perfect way to describe the Seder night. It is a complex adventure, full of rituals and food, songs and storytelling. There's matzah—a unique unleavened flatbread that hasn't been allowed time to rise. There's the Seder Plate—a collection of foods, each with their own meaning and purpose. And there's the Haggadah—a book of instructions and traditions, laid out in more than a dozen steps.

One of those steps contains the Four Questions, a famous bit of text (often read or sung by children) that asks why this night is different from all others. *On all other nights*, the Haggadah says, we do things one way; why on this night are things changed?

The answer is the *story*. In every generation, questions are asked. Stories are told. That's the heart of the Passover Seder. And it's the heart of this book, too.

On All Other Nights is an anthology of short stories, each inspired by one of the steps of the Seder, presented in the traditional order. We have fiction and nonfiction. Stories from the past and stories from now. Realistic stories and fantasy. A story in verse. A graphic story. We all write differently. And we also come from different traditions, different backgrounds, different homes. But we're here at this table to share our stories with one another—and with you.

We hope you find something here that reminds you of yourself. We also hope you find something that doesn't. Because now we are free—free to speak, free to listen, free to ask questions. Even free to disagree. We might not all be the same. But that doesn't mean we can't sit at the same table. And read the same book.

Whether you're Jewish or not, whether you celebrate Passover or not, whether you're reading this in spring or some other time of year—welcome to our table. We are so happy to have you.

Let all who are hungry come and read.

So much love,
Chris, Josh, and Naomi

HOW IS THIS ANTHOLOGY DIFFERENT FROM ALL OTHER ANTHOLOGIES?

As mentioned in the introduction, each of the following stories is inspired by one of the steps of the Seder. We leave it to you to discover those connections, some more obvious than others.

To help in your journey, before each story, we have added a description of each step, followed by—what else?—four questions. These questions may connect to the step, or the story, but mostly, we hope they connect with you.

KADESH

The first step of the Seder is called Kadesh, a short prayer recited over a cup of wine or grape juice—one of four filled throughout the night. The word "Kadesh" comes from a Hebrew word that means "separation." It's a boundary, a starting line. An action that says: Something has ended, but something else is about to begin.

- *How does it feel to start something new—join a new school, make a new friend, find a new home?*

- *Have you tried something new lately? Taken on any new responsibility? How did it go? Will you try it again?*

- *If you could invent your own ritual to mark the beginning of something, what would it be, and why?*

- *Kadesh marks the start of the Seder. But for many who celebrate Passover, there is a lot that comes before: Cooking for the meal. Ridding the home of bread and other "leavened" food called "chametz" (some even burn the chametz, too). Lighting candles. Not everyone does everything. But getting ready for Passover is often a kind of ritual all to itself. Have you ever looked forward to a really special day? What did you do to prepare?*

BREAKING BREAD AT THE SEDER

BY MARI LOWE

There are scales of trouble when you're twelve. There's *forgot your homework at home* trouble, which is pretty minor, as far as Yossi is concerned. Maybe he'd have to sit out recess or get a mark in a teacher's roll book. There's *pinched Menachem because he wouldn't stop shrieking in your ear* trouble, which might get him an aggravated lecture and some minor punishment.

Then there's the other kind of trouble, the one that's in the league of *accidentally locked everyone out of the house right before a family event* or, more recently, *snuck out of school during gym and went to the pizza store down the block*, which had earned Yossi a week's grounding and a month on litter box duty.

Yeah, that's the kind of trouble he's in right now, on the night before Pesach, when they're searching the house for leftover chametz crumbs that they might have missed. A month ago, there had been chametz everywhere—crumbled bread in the toy box, a cracker under Shevy's crib, a suspiciously half-eaten package of Oreos in Ahuva's underwear drawer. Over the last few weeks, they'd scrubbed everything clean. There couldn't be *anything* chametz left in the house. Tatty says that on a holiday when they celebrate the liberation of the Jews, they get rid of chametz to remind them that they are supposed to be humble like matzah instead of puffed-up and arrogant like bread. Mommy says that they might as well do some spring cleaning while they're at it, and don't you think that the bookcases could use a good dusting?

Now that they're in the middle of the final hunt for chametz, though, they're doing what is usually Yossi's favorite part of the search. It's an old tradition that everyone he knows follows. They hide ten pieces of bread, each of them just about the size and shape of a folded dollar bill and wrapped securely in silver foil so no crumbs can escape into their pristinely chametz-free house. Officially, it's so that their search won't be in vain. Unofficially, it's just *fun*. The Rosenfelds next door like to put their hidden pieces in the same places every year. Mommy tries to change it up, but she's become predictable. Yossi and Ahuva had protested this year, and Yossi, as the oldest, finally snagged the job of hiding them.

Had Tatty said, "Yossi, don't forget to write down where you hide them, just in case," earlier that day? Yes. Had Yossi forgotten his father's reminder in the excitement of picking the perfect hiding spots? Also yes.

It's just that he gets distracted sometimes, and little details like *keep track of where you hide chametz the night before Pesach* drift away in the face of something more exciting. It's why Mommy had suggested that Ahuva hide them instead. Yossi had protested, had pointed out that he was older and it was his turn, and had seized the bag of bread before Ahuva could snatch it away.

As the next-to-oldest, Ahuva had led the search party, peering into the backs of cabinets and taking apart a game box of *Settlers of Catan* to find one. Menachem had crawled under beds, and Shevy had climbed onto the treadmill in a death-defying act of recklessness, and they'd managed to track down nearly every piece of Yossi's bread—except for that last one, which had been in such a forgettable spot that now, an hour into the search, Yossi has no idea where he put it.

So, yeah, it's the night before Pesach and Yossi has hidden chametz in some impossible location, and he's about to be in *huge* trouble. Mommy is going to panic. Tatty is never going to trust him with something like this again. The pit in Yossi's stomach churns at the realization.

Ahuva emerges from inside a hamper in the bathroom, her dark hair tangled in the white strings of someone's tzitzis, and says, "Not in here. I think I'm ready to give up."

Yossi bobs his head. "Cool. That's cool. I'll just . . . go do my grand reveal of where I hid the final piece of chametz. It's in the last spot you'd expect. A stroke of genius from me, really. As the family genius."

Ahuva narrows her eyes at him. "You have no clue where it is."

Yossi winces. "Look," he says, opting for superiority instead of terror and dread. "You're ten. You can't be expected to be as good as I was last year. You're just a kid."

"You were barely eleven last year," Ahuva says, unimpressed. "Did you write it down like Tatty told you to?" She looks gleeful at his expression. "Oh, boy. You're in *trouble*."

Yossi grits his teeth. Nothing makes him quite as cranky as begging Ahuva for help. She always finds a way to cash in on his debts in the worst possible way, and she's sneaky in a way that he's never mastered. On the other hand, *sneaky* might be his only hope right now. "Ahuva," he says pleadingly. "I'll owe you."

Menachem watches them negotiate with great interest. Shevy entertains herself by squirting toothpaste into the sink in bright green loops. Tatty calls from downstairs, "Yossi! Ahuva! Wrap it up."

Ahuva smirks. "You are *so* lucky that you have me." She strides downstairs, the others tumbling behind her, and she ducks into the kitchen while Yossi watches. The kitchen is all ready for Pesach. The table has been covered with sticky paper, and the counters have hard white plastic over them. Cabinets have been taped closed, and the stove is coated in foil. It's all there to make sure that none of their Pesach food touches chametz, and Yossi has ruined everything by losing a whole piece of *bread* somewhere in the house.

Ahuva wanders over to the stove and peels off a piece of tape from the edge of it.

"What are you doing?" Yossi whispers, horrified. Ahuva puts a finger to her lips and rips a strip of foil, too. She folds the tape into a loose square just as Mommy walks into the kitchen.

Mommy's eyes go wide at the sight of the brown bag full of bread pieces that Menachem is holding. "Out!" she orders. "Out, out, with that chametz!" They scamper from the room, Ahuva folding her foil over the tape, and she slips the final piece of wrapped foil into the bag.

"That doesn't help," Yossi hisses to her. "The chametz is still missing."

"It buys us time," Ahuva retorts. "And it saves you from having to tell Tatty that he was right about you. Do you want my help or not?" Yossi freezes, and Ahuva says in a singsong, "Tatty, I can't find—"

Yossi cringes. "OK!" He grits his teeth. "Just don't—"

"Never mind!" Ahuva calls, emerging into the dining room where Tatty is still waiting. "Found it!" She passes the bag to Tatty with a winning smile. Tatty counts the pieces, drops them into the bag, satisfied, and sends them all to bed.

9

Yossi lies in bed, listening to the sounds of his parents cooking downstairs. Mommy sautés onions while Tatty coats chicken with potato chips and fries it, and they talk about what they're preparing for the Seder tomorrow night. The two Seder nights are Yossi's favorite nights of the year. Sure, Magid is so long sometimes that his eyes glaze over and he starts throwing chocolate chips at Ahuva from across the table, but he likes the singing and the talking, the discussions that arise and the animal noises that everyone who's still awake at the end makes while they sing Chad Gadya.

He can't ruin it by losing that piece of bread. He's going to have to find it, or he'll have to admit the truth to everyone. They can't go into Pesach with a piece of bread hidden in the house, and—even worse—Yossi will have to admit that he didn't follow Tatty's advice.

Telling Tatty will be even worse than owing Ahuva a favor. Tatty is the kind of person who's always on time, who writes down everything he has to do on a list, and who probably never wore yesterday's filthy pants to school when he was a kid. Yossi is disorganized and forgetful and easily distracted, and he's sure that this will be yet another time that he earns a scolding and that *look* from Tatty, the one that means that Yossi has disappointed him again.

And the worst part is, his parents are never going to give him any kind of responsibility again. More and more lately, he's been treated like an adult—or at least a *teenager*, some-one who can go out on his own to run errands and who doesn't need a parent checking on his homework and who hangs out with the adults sometimes when all the other kids have run away from the Shabbos table.

He *has* to do better this time.

He waits until Menachem's breathing is even and quiet in the bottom bunk, then he slips down the ladder silently and tiptoes from his room. He squeezes his eyes shut, try-ing to visualize the moment when he'd hidden each piece of chametz. *There*, he'd slipped one into the bathroom, under the plunger that sits beside the toilet. *There*, he'd wedged one under a slat of the bunk bed. *There*, one had been tucked into Ahuva's jewelry box.

Ahuva had found all of those. Which one is still missing?

Carefully, he creeps down to the ground floor, and he's almost there when Mommy says suddenly, "Is that someone on the stairs?"

Yossi flings himself over the side of the railing without a second thought, landing on the opposite side of the stair-case. He's in the dining room now, flattened beside a stack of folding chairs. He can see through the cracks of the chairs that Mommy is peering around the room. She shrugs and turns back. "Think that was the cat," she says, returning to where she's grating the maror that they'll eat at the Seder, eyes red from the pungent scent.

Tatty laughs. "Better the cat than one of the kids," he says. "I have this nightmare that Shevy is going to grab the bag of chametz from the front door tomorrow morning and unwrap all of the bread. Remember what she did when she was two?"

"That was a couple of years ago," Mommy reminds him. "The kids are growing up. Yossi even hid the bread this year, and that went off without a hitch."

Yossi gulps. There is a new sensation rising through him when he thinks about the missing bread. It isn't just panic anymore; there's guilt, too, because he really *is* getting older and he's too old to have done something this *stupid*.

Carefully, he steals past his parents, darting down the stairs to the basement. He knows he came down here to hide some of the bread. There had been one in a Lego fortress, and another was . . .

He doesn't remember, but his eyes flicker down the dark hall to the storage closet at the end of it and he shudders. It's creepy down here. He can't turn on the light without turning on all the lights in the basement, all the way to the stairs where Tatty might see. He'll have to go in without any light.

He starts forward with slow, heavy steps, his heart pounding in his chest. Outside, the wind howls so loudly that Yossi can hear it from the basement. The street cats are yowling, and the carpet seems to shift as he walks, like a dozen spiders are creeping across it. Yossi doesn't want to go any farther.

Yossi doesn't have a *choice*. Carefully, he moves deeper into the dark, until he can finally creak the closet door open and move his hands around on the shelf, searching for a glint of silver foil. His breath sounds loud and ragged, and he's suddenly sure that he can hear rustling in the closet, something else moving just below him—

A hand flashes in the dark, light and quick, and seizes his elbow. Yossi screams, and a second hand closes over his mouth. "Be quiet!" Ahuva's voice hisses behind him. Yossi snaps his teeth at Ahuva's palm, but she dodges away, agile and swift. "Do you want us to get caught?"

"What are you doing here?" Yossi demands in a low voice, his heart still beating rapidly.

Ahuva blinks at him. "Searching for the chametz, *duh*. I'm not going to let us go into Pesach with chametz still in the house. But I didn't find anything here." She has a tiny handheld flashlight that she moves around in a swooping motion, and Yossi snatches it.

"We need to check everywhere," he says, directing the flashlight at the far corner of the storage closet. "I remember coming back here."

"Yeah. You put one inside a paper towel roll," Ahuva says, pointing to the big package of paper towels. "I found that one right away. As the family genius." She grabs her flashlight back. "You think you'd hide two here?"

Yossi doesn't know. Hiding the chametz feels like a dim memory now, like something he's tried too hard to touch and now can't access at all. Did he drop a piece of bread along the way? Is it just in a corner somewhere?

They check every last inch of the basement, including such highlights as: Ahuva wedged behind the couch, legs waving wildly in the air as she hisses, "I'm stuck! I'm stuck!"; Yossi digging through the litter box with a shovel as the cat watches with great mistrust; and both of them climbing up the washing machine to check the rafters.

"I feel like I would remember if I'd climbed up there," Yossi says ruefully after they make the jump down. So far, they've found a rotten apple in Shevy's dollhouse, a rotten cucumber in Shevy's puzzle box, and a rotten peach between the couch cushions under one of Shevy's books. "Right now, the only thing I know is that Shevy needs to learn how to use a garbage can."

"No chametz," Ahuva says glumly.

"No chametz," Yossi agrees. "It must be upstairs."

But upstairs, Mommy and Tatty are setting the dining room table for the Seder. There's no way that Yossi is going to be able to check the ground floor, so they wait until their parents are in the kitchen, backs turned, and quietly make their way upstairs.

"We'll find it," Yossi says, but he believes it less and less now.

This is a disaster. His parents are never going to trust him again. Tatty is going to shake his head, that same old *what did we expect?* And Yossi will have no defense.

He thinks about lying, about keeping it from his parents, but he knows that he'd get caught and then it'll be even worse. Mommy has a sixth sense for Yossi's guilty conscience, and he'll never be able to hide it forever. Besides, Menachem and Shevy heard it all, and who knows what they might say tomorrow?

But no one says a word in the morning. When Yossi staggers out of bed, bleary-eyed from lack of sleep, Mommy only says, "Hurry and get dressed. We're going to get bagels before we burn the chametz."

The day is a whirlwind from there, no time to make grand confessions or even launch another search. They eat bagels on the front lawn, chasing after stray napkins. Then they dust themselves off and drop their garbage into the metal can in the driveway. The last stage of getting rid of chametz is burning anything that they still have so it's completely inedible. Tatty has filled the can with old wood and cardboard boxes, and he sets it on fire as he reads the Kol Chamira in Aramaic, and then in English. "Any chametz that I didn't find, see, or know about should become like the dust of the earth," he says aloud, and Yossi repeats it, a nasty knot in his stomach.

Tatty empties ten pieces of foil with nine pieces of bread into the can, and then he beckons Yossi over. "Go ahead," he says, and he offers Yossi a warm smile. "You can help stoke the fire. You're old enough." Yossi pushes at the fire with a stick, but he doesn't enjoy it nearly as much as he might have a day ago. Instead, he thinks about the missing bread and is too ashamed to crow to Ahuva about this new responsibility.

After that, they head back inside to clean their rooms for Pesach and take a nap. Yossi has never actually slept during a pre-Pesach nap, and he plans to use this one to search for the bread some more. Technically, it should be gone already, but at least finding it now would be better than finding it on Pesach itself.

But when he stretches out in bed, he falls fast asleep, exhausted from the drama of last night, and when he wakes up, it's time to eat a late lunch and prepare for the Seder.

He glances around the dining room desperately as he helps set up the Seder Plate, as though that tenth piece might appear out of nowhere. But still, there is no bread, and soon he has to leave for shul and give up on the bread entirely.

Ahuva shoots him a panicked look as he leaves, and he shrugs helplessly. It's too late now to tell Mommy and Tatty. At least they don't know about it. It's just Yossi's problem now.

And Ahuva's, a little bit, and he fully intends to remind her of that again when he gets back from shul. That's the advantage to having a sister, isn't it? He doesn't have to carry this alone. They share their messes.

He walks home from shul with Tatty. The streets are thronged with people, all of them streaming out of shuls in new clothes and shoes, and Yossi sees a few of his friends and waves. Tatty greets everyone he knows along the way, and Yossi's guilt wavers against the force of his impatience. Tonight won't be quite what he imagined it would be, but it is the Seder, and the panic begins to fade, to be replaced with excitement.

Inside, the house is gleaming clean, with dishes on the table that they use for only these eight days of the year. Every chair has a pillow, and each kid has a special kiddush cup at their place for their four cups of grape juice. Ahuva is handing out the haggadahs that they'll read aloud from during the Seder, and Tatty and Menachem belt out the song for the order of the Seder together.

Yossi sets aside his dread and brings his haggadah to his seat, vowing to forget about his mess with the chametz. Maybe he won't find the bread at all. It's not a problem if you don't find the chametz on Pesach, right?

And with that cheery thought, he stands next to his seat and turns the haggadah to Kadesh. He fills Tatty's cup with wine, and Tatty fills Yossi's with grape juice, and it feels as though everything is going to be just fine.

Tatty pulls on his white fabric kittel, the robe that he wears for the Seder, and he lifts his cup and clears his throat to begin. And then he frowns. "That's strange," he says. "There's something in the pocket of my kittel."

And—*oh no, oh no, oh no*—Yossi remembers. The kittel had been draped across Tatty's chair last night, ready for the Seder, and Yossi had stuck a piece of chametz into the front pocket without a second thought, such a spontaneous decision that he'd been distracted a moment later and forgotten about it.

Tatty pulls the piece of foil out of his pocket, just the size and shape of a dollar bill, and Yossi's heart thumps in his ribs like it might burst.

Ahuva says without missing a beat, "Wow, Yossi, did you hide an eleventh piece of chametz? Not cool." Yossi contemplates jumping onto the table to strangle her.

Tatty says disapprovingly, "Of course, he didn't. Our Yossi's a straight shooter. This must be something else." He begins to unwrap the foil, directly over the kiddush cup filled with wine, and Yossi can't *do* this, can't handle this—

"It's the tenth piece!" he says in a rush. "I *know*, I didn't write them down, and we couldn't find it—we searched all night—I didn't know how to tell you—*please*, Tatty, don't open it—"

Tatty shakes his head slowly. "Yossi," he says, and he heaves a sigh. "I'm very disappointed in you." And he unwraps the foil.

Yossi watches in horror—sees the flash of white—

And Tatty pulls out four marshmallows—white and fluffy and very much not chametz—from the foil. "Mostly, I'm disappointed that you think I didn't know what you were up to," he says, and Yossi stares at him in disbelief. Tatty raises his eyebrows at Yossi. "I found the chametz when I tried on my kittel last night, while you and Ahuva were making enough noise in the basement to wake the dead. I stuck it into the bag before we burned the chametz."

Yossi gapes at him. Tatty grins. "Come on, Yossi. Never underestimate your father when it comes to food." There is no reproof on his face, and Yossi doesn't *understand*—shouldn't he be in trouble? Tatty says, "It's a rite of passage, losing the chametz. I did it when I was nine, I remember," he says thoughtfully. "Didn't find it until I got into bed and saw it taped to the top of the bunk bed."

"*You* lost the chametz?" Yossi blurts out. He can't imagine Tatty—always so neat, always so organized—ever losing track of something that important.

Tatty raises his eyebrows. "I used to lose everything. Why do you think I'm always making lists?" He shakes his head, and that *look* comes onto his face again. Stunned, Yossi sees it for what it really is: *recognition*. "It's the only way I can keep track of things. You might want to start doing it, too," he says, a mild reproof that Yossi takes without question. "And next time, I'd like to hear about something like this before the Seder."

"Next time, I think *I* should hide the chametz," Ahuva pipes up, and Tatty laughs.

"Maybe in a few years," he says. "But I think Yossi should get another chance to do it right, don't you?" Yossi can feel the knot in his stomach untying, his breath evening out. Tatty lays a hand on his shoulder. "We can talk about it some other time," he says, and he nods to Mommy's amused face, to Shevy banging a plastic spoon on her haggadah, to Ahuva and Menachem and Yossi himself. "Right now, I'd rather we all just enjoy the Seder."

He tosses a marshmallow to each of them—first Shevy, then Menachem, then Ahuva, then straight at Yossi's nose—and lifts his kiddush cup. "Now," he says, and Yossi exhales, relieved and abashed and very glad to return to the Seder. "Let's begin."

URCHATZ

Hand-washing. That's it. That's the step. No special words are recited. No soap is used. It's simply water poured from a cup over fingers. This is the first of two times hands are washed during the Seder—and one of many parts of the Haggadah whose purpose is a bit mysterious. Is it for cleanliness? Symbolism? Memory of an ancient custom no longer widely practiced? Or maybe . . . it's just so we have a reason to ask: *Why?*

- *Why do you think the second step of the Seder is a simple washing of the hands?*

- *Water appears quite a lot in the Exodus story, which begins with the Egyptian Pharaoh enslaving the Jews and wanting all Jewish baby boys thrown in the Nile (water). One family saves their child by sending him in a basket down the river (water). He is rescued by a princess, who names him Moses, which—according to the story—means, "I drew him from the water." Moses is raised in the Egyptian palace but grows up to save his people. Through Moses, God sends the Ten Plagues on the Egyptians, beginning with turning the Nile (water) to blood. The Jews are eventually freed, but not before the Egyptian army gives chase—across a sea (water) split open so the Jews can pass on dry land. Why do you think water appears so much in this story? What might it mean?*

- *Can you think of any other story—a book, a movie, a game, anything—where water also appears? Did it mean something there, too?*

- *Is there anything that you do—or that your family does—because it was done by people who came before you? Just because? How does that make you feel?*

THE TRUTH ABOUT THE MERMAIDS

BY R.M. ROMERO

Isabel's Abuelita liked to say everyone had their own Egypt.

Sometimes, Egypt was a *place* they were running from, where the rivers were deep blue with sadness and the sky was red with fear. Sometimes, Egypt was a *person* with rough hands and even harsher words who wanted to grab them by the ankles and make them do what they were told.

Sometimes, it was both.

Abuelita's Egypt was Havana, where the buildings were as colorful as parakeets and everyone spoke two languages: Spanish on the street and secrets in their houses. She told her family about her escape from Havana every Passover during the Seder, before the family washed their hands for the first time.

For Isabel, her grandmother's story was tangled up in Moses's flight from Egypt. He parted one sea so he and his people could walk to freedom, and Abuelita sailed across another in search of her own.

"*Habia una vez,*" Abuelita began, because all the best tales must start with "once upon a time," "I lived in a kingdom ruled by a wizard with a beard as long as a lie. His name was Castro, and he wanted everyone to live in a world where time stood still. But many people didn't want to live in the wizard's never-ending past. They shuffled their feet in new dances and sang new songs and painted new things. They wrote new books and invented new medicines. The wizard tolerated this . . . until the people of the island decided they wanted to leave his old and crumbling kingdom.

"My family and I—my mother and my father and my little brother, Camilo—decided that we should leave, too. There wasn't enough food to go around and our bellies were almost always empty in those days, but our hearts and minds were full with dreams and love for each other.

"'We will go to the United States, where we will always have enough of everything,' my mother promised.

"So one night, the four of us went down to the Havana Harbor. We outraced the moonlight until we reached my father's little fishing boat. As our parents loaded parcels of food and jugs of water into it, Camilo clung to me the way music notes cling to the air. 'I'm scared of sailing out to sea,' he whispered.

"I wrapped my arms around him tight. 'You don't need to be afraid. We're islanders! The ocean is our friend.'

"'But what about storms? What about sharks?'

"I hoisted Camilo onto my hip and ruffled his curls with

a grin I only half meant. Secretly, I was worried, too. 'What about sunshine?' I countered. 'What about mermaids?'

"Camilo wrinkled his nose. 'Mermaids aren't real.'

"'Just because you haven't seen something doesn't make it not real,' I said. 'The realest things of all aren't always the ones we can touch.'

"My brother studied me with eyes as dark as the water lapping at the sides of our boat. He must have been thinking hard about what I'd told him. 'Maybe we'll see a mermaid then,' he finally said, 'on our way to the United States.'

"I forced myself to smile. 'Maybe we will.'

"Hidden by the night, our fishing boat snuck out of the harbor. We held our breath as Havana faded into the darkness. We weren't followed by sailors from the wizard's coast guard, the way my parents had feared we might be. But we were followed by one of Camilo's fears: a storm!"

Abuelita grabbed the corners of the table and shook it, like the ghost of Elijah the prophet had arrived at the Seder early to drink his glass of wine. It was a good way to make everyone feel like they were inside the story, the way the whole Seder made Isabel feel like she was walking away from Egypt alongside Moses and Miriam and the other Israelites. But at the end of the night, she always settled back into reality.

"The rain and the wind threatened to sweep us away!" Abuelita continued. "We clung—to the sides of the boat and to one another. I'd never hated the ocean before! But in that moment, I did. The sea stood like a soldier between my family and the life we wanted. And little by little, it began to steal from us.

"It grabbed the ship's sail and ripped it away! It smashed the boat's rudder against a cluster of rocks! It battered me and my family so much that we started to believe we'd never be dry and warm again.

"Then the sea stole me and Camilo.

"One moment, I was holding my mother's hand and my brother was holding mine . . . and the next, Camilo and I were tumbling through the rough water. The waves slammed into us over and over again, drowning out the cries of our parents as they tried to steer the boat back to us.

"I found Camilo in the dark and begged him, 'Swim! Swim!'

"But no matter how fast or hard we kicked our legs and flailed our arms, we could barely keep our heads above the waves! Just as I feared I was going to sink and I began to whisper the Shema, something—or rather, *someone*—grabbed me and Camilo."

Here, Abuelita paused and closed her eyes for a moment, as if she needed to dive deeper into the memory to finish her story. Then she whispered, "Our rescuer was a mermaid, her rainbow tail arching from the water.

"Camilo screamed—and the mermaid hushed him like a lullaby. 'Be still! I'm here to help both of you. I won't let you drown,' she said in perfect Spanish. Or maybe by then, I'd learned to speak the language of the howling wind. 'Like the two of you, I once tried to cross the ocean and start a new life. I didn't make it. But I want you to.'

"Despite the water striking my face, I made myself focus on the mermaid: the tangle of her hair, her bronze skin, the dimples at the corners of her mouth. She could have been my mother or my grandmother; she could have been me in a few years. She was human . . . and at the same time, she wasn't.

"She was the kinder, softer part of the sea. The part that carried people to safety.

"'I trust you,' I said to the mermaid.

"'I trust you, too,' Camilo echoed.

"The mermaid was strong—stronger than even the current. The water tried to push the three of us under again and again. She pushed back and swam on, past the night and the thunder, and into the dawn. When the sun finally rose, the ocean was glass-still once again, and the sky had turned back into its usual, welcoming blue.

"And there, on the horizon, was a golden beach with an enormous stone fort behind it. It was Fort Jefferson, in the United States of America, and it was waiting for me and Camilo. Our family's fishing boat lay on its side in the sand, and I knew our parents must be waiting for us, too.

"The mermaid let go of me and my brother. The water was

so calm and shallow now that it barely lapped at my waist and Camilo's sunburned shoulders.

"'When you take your first step onto the sand,' said the mermaid, 'you'll be free.'

"'And what about you?' Camilo asked.

"The mermaid smiled. 'There are always storms and people who get caught in them. I'll be busy. But maybe we'll meet someday—if you're in need of rescue again.' Then she plunged back into the deeper water, her tail a shimmer under the gentle waves.

"Camilo waved. 'Goodbye!' he cried. 'Thank you!'

"'Goodbye,' I said softly.

"We watched the mermaid fade away, like all good dreams must eventually. When she was gone, I took Camilo's hand. We waded to shore together, purple with bruises, but neither of us hesitated. We each took a long breath, stepped out of the sea . . . and walked into our new lives."

Everyone at the table remained quiet for a long time after.

It was Isabel who broke the silence. As the youngest child at the Seder, she always asked the Four Questions. But this time, she asked a fifth. Because while she might still *be* the youngest, Isabel was also old enough not to believe in mermaids anymore. "It's a good story, Abuelita. But how did you *really* get to the United States with Gran Tío Camilo after you both got thrown overboard?" she asked.

Abuelita sighed at her granddaughter. "Weren't you listening to anything I just told you?"

"I was!" Isabel huffed. "But mermaids aren't real. Somebody else must have saved you."

"Rashi the sage believed in mermaids, and he was very wise," Abuelita pointed out.

Isabel rolled her eyes. "Rashi was born in 1040—and he studied Torah, not science," she replied. "He probably thought the Earth was the center of the universe and narwhals were unicorns, like everybody else did back then."

Abuelita winked. "You should become a rabbi. You like asking questions even when it's not Passover . . . and having arguments."

"I'm not arguing," said Isabel, although she was doing just that. "I just can't believe in magic without some kind of proof! My teachers say that people used myths like mermaids and monsters to explain stuff they didn't understand. That doesn't make those myths *real*."

"There are some things that we just have to believe in, whether or not we have proof that they existed outside of a memory," Abuelita told her. "That's what the Seder's all about, isn't it? Memories of the past guiding us into new beginnings."

Isabel sunk lower in her seat. She loved Abuelita; she even loved Abuelita's story and the spell it cast over the glasses of wine and bowls of charoset made of dates and cinnamon and fresh oranges. Yet Isabel knew it was only a fairy tale dipped in salt water and history.

Maybe the mermaid had been a kind boat captain who had caught Abuelita and Gran Tío Camilo in her net. Maybe the mermaid was Abuelita herself, the girl who'd defied a storm and Castro, the man who thought he was a wizard. But whoever the rescuer was, Isabel decided she *had* to have been human.

It was this thought that stuck to Isabel the way the sand stuck to the bottoms of her feet as she made her way down to the beach beside her family's apartment the next morning. The grown-ups were sleeping in; they usually did the morning after the Seder.

Isabel wriggled out of her T-shirt and kicked her sandals off. She ignored the red flags flapping on the sides of the nearest lifeguard tower that meant no one was on duty, and how the waves smashed angrily against her knees as she stepped into the ocean.

"Why won't Abuelita tell me the *real* truth?" Isabel muttered as she began to paddle through the water. "I'm old enough to know and I'm tired of fairy tales. I—"

Isabel never had the chance to finish her complaint. The outgoing tide wrapped itself around her ankles . . . and pulled her under. Isabel tried to grab at the ocean floor to stop herself from being yanked out to sea, but the sand slipped through her fingers.

She let out a muffled scream as the tide carried her farther and farther away from the beach, from her parents and Abuelita and every friend she'd ever had. Beneath the surface, there was nothing except blue darkness . . . and it seemed to go on forever.

Until, that is, something broke through it: a long, thin shadow. It came toward Isabel with frightening speed, hurtling closer and closer with every breath she tried to take. Isabel squeezed her eyes shut and waited for the flare of pain that was sure to come as a shark closed its jaws around her.

Instead, she felt a pair of strong arms embrace her. *Human* arms.

Isabel's eyes snapped open. The world was still a blur of midnight blue, but it was getting brighter by the moment as she and the stranger rose up into the light. They broke the surface and Isabel dragged down gulp after greedy gulp of air.

"Are you all right?" her rescuer asked, thumping Isabel's back. She was a beautiful young woman, sunlight tucked in the corners of her smile, dark hair dripping into her eyes. She wasn't wearing a lifeguard's red swimsuit or a silver whistle, but that didn't mean much. Like Isabel and Abuelita, she could be an islander.

And islanders knew how to swim better than anyone.

Isabel couldn't answer the stranger yet. It felt like the entire ocean had tried to sneak inside of her, and she spit out a mouthful of seawater, coughing. Finally, she managed to croak, "I'm OK . . . I think."

The stranger smiled. "Good! I'm glad you're all right. But next time, don't go swimming so far out when the tides are this angry."

Isabel rubbed at her stinging eyes. The world was still a little blurry at the edges, and she squinted at the stranger, trying—without much success—to bring her into focus. "The tides can get angry?"

"Even on a good day, they have a temper," said the stranger. "Although I think they'd be much less angry if you humans stopped throwing all your garbage into the sea."

"Humans? I don't . . ." Isabel's gaze traveled from the top of the stranger's head down to where her legs should have been kicking as wildly as Isabel's were. But the woman had no legs.

She had a *tail*.

Its scales came in a sunset splash of color—all bright yellows and oranges—and it ended in two silky pink fins. The stranger was impossible in every way.

But so was escaping Egypt. Any Egypt.

"I'm dreaming," Isabel whispered. "Or I really did drown."

"You didn't drown. I promise." The mermaid—that was the only thing she could have been—tilted her head to the side, peering more closely at Isabel. "Do I know you?" She leaned in, her nose brushing against Isabel's. "You look very familiar."

"I've never seen you before," said Isabel. "I've never seen anything *like* you!"

The mermaid laughed. "Yes, you have. I *do* know you. I saved you once before! I've never saved anyone twice."

"You couldn't have! I . . ." But Isabel's denial unraveled like the fringes of her father's prayer shawl. "Wait . . . You must have known my *grandmother*! You must be the one who rescued her!"

"Your grandmother?" The mermaid flicked her forever-damp hair over one shoulder and considered. "I suppose that makes sense," she said after a pause. "I sometimes forget that humans age much faster than I do. But I was right about you looking familiar."

Isabel nodded. The feeling that she'd slipped into a dream hadn't left her yet. She wondered if it ever would . . . and if this was how Abuelita had felt when she'd been with the mermaid.

"Do you think you can get to shore on your own?" the mermaid asked. "The sea seems calmer now."

Isabel glanced back at the beach. A growing mosaic of umbrellas and towels was forming on the sand as more and more people left their condos and hotels to bask in the sun. Few of them ventured into the water; they'd probably paid more attention to the red flags than Isabel had.

"I think so," she said carefully. "Are you going to stay?"

"I'll be a little farther out. But I'll be close by." The mermaid smacked the water with the end of her tail, sighing.

"You never know about the ocean—it could decide to throw another temper tantrum. It needs to get better at expressing how it feels."

Isabel nodded. Then, knowing words weren't enough, she said softly, "Thank you for saving me."

"You're welcome," the mermaid replied. "Tell your grandmother I said hello."

Before Isabel could promise she would, the mermaid slipped back under the water, becoming little more than a sparkling blur of color. Isabel waved in farewell, as her Gran Tío Camilo had done all those years before.

With the mermaid now out of sight, Isabel swam slowly back to shore, mindful of how the sea shifted around her. Her thoughts felt like a whirlpool, all swirling together, as she climbed out of the water. Trying to steady herself, Isabel headed up the beach to the public showers. She turned one on and stood underneath it, letting the cold water bring her back to herself—and her new life. It was a life where magic was hidden in every breaking wave.

As she rubbed the salt and sand off her hands, Isabel realized that no one on the beach knew what had happened to her that day. And she doubted that any of the tourists or the sunbathers or even her best friends would believe her if she told them.

But as she shook the water from her hair, Isabel realized there was one person who *would* believe her. That person

knew *every* story held more than just a whisper of truth—
whether or not there was any proof of it outside of memory.

Isabel looked back at the sea. "I should go talk to Abuelita,"
she said. "I think she'll want to hear *my* story about mermaids
this time."

KARPAS

The third step of the Seder is called Karpas. A vegetable—sometimes parsley, celery, or potato—is dipped in salt water and eaten. The water symbolizes tears and helps us remember the slavery in Egypt, called Mitzrayim in Hebrew. Some dip green vegetables, maybe as a symbol of springtime and hope. Others use root vegetables, maybe to help us remember our roots, where we've come from, and what we're connected to.

- *Which kind of vegetable would you dip for Karpas, and why?*

- *Karpas is one of the special foods placed on the Seder Plate, alongside maror (a bitter herb, reminding us of the bitterness of the slavery in Egypt), charoset (a sweet mixture, often of fruit and nuts, reminding us of the bricks the Jews used to build), and other foods. There are many different Seder Plate traditions. If you could set a plate with several foods to remember a special event in your life, what would those foods be and why?*

- *Tears are often sad—but not always. Can you think of a time you shed happy tears?*

- *Can you think of a story that means something to you, something you'd want to remember, even though it makes you feel sad? Maybe it's a story from real life. Maybe it's fiction. Now invent a ritual that helps you remember.*

CHOCOLATE TEARS

BY NAOMI MILLINER

This year, I'd rather pass on Passover.

One of the things I loved most about the holiday was that I always knew what to expect, that it was always the same, one year to the next.

I loved making Passover rolls and matzoh toffee with my mom. I loved searching everywhere for the afikoman with my brothers while Dad told us if we were "hot" or "cold." I loved that every year my oldest brother, Jordan, ate too much horseradish and coughed 'til he cried (and the rest of us tried not to laugh). And I loved that, when we got to the songs at the end, everyone took a part (or two) for Chad Gadya, and my little brother, Izzy, always played "the kid"— since he's the youngest.

But this year, even if every one of those things happens, it *won't* be the same.

This year, I really do want to pass on Passover.

❧

I burrow under my covers with my favorite book, *Little Women*. Grandma Clara gave it to me a year and a half ago for my tenth birthday. Even though it was written in the 1860s,

Jo March and her three sisters aren't all that different from girls today.

My grandmother was one of four daughters, too, which is why she loved this book growing up. Then she and her sisters had ten children between them: all boys. It looked like all the grandkids would be boys, too—until I came along.

Before I get lost in Jo's world, I reach for another comfort item: chocolate.

My family and I are obsessed with it: gooey brownies, hot fudge sundaes, creamy French silk pie—even salted chocolate caramel sauce. Since the only chocolate in my room is a candy bar, it'll have to do.

I'm a few pages into the chapter, and a few bites into the candy bar, when there's a knock on my door.

"Rachel?"

Before I can say "come in" (or don't), my six-year-old brother, Izzy (short for Isaac), invites himself in.

"Izzy! You're supposed to wait for me to say OK," I remind him for the hundredth time.

"Why?"

Before I can even answer, he keeps talking.

"Mommy called." Izzy hops onto my bed and squeezes in next to me, freckled cheeks, missing front tooth, and all. "She said Mrs. Keller's baby is being stubborn, so she asked us to start getting ready without her."

"Start getting ready without Mrs. Keller?" I ask, knowing that's not what he means.

As expected, Izzy laughs. "Without Mommy, silly."

"Are you calling Mommy silly?"

He laughs some more. "No! You're silly! Mommy can't leave the hospital 'til the baby comes out."

"Oh, OK." I put my butterfly bookmark between the pages and follow him downstairs to the kitchen, where our fifteen-year-old brother, Dylan, is already hard at work.

Dylan's side of the table is cluttered with a carton of eggs, bottles of club soda and olive oil, a box of matzoh meal, a container of kosher salt, and three mixing bowls of various sizes. This can mean only one thing . . .

"Making matzoh balls already?" I ask.

He looks over at me. "I've been thinking how ironic it is that all over the world, Jews celebrate a holiday about free-dom by spending all day—or longer—doing a ton of work."

"It's not work," Izzy says. "It's fun!"

And he's right; at least, it used to be . . .

"Fun, huh?" Dylan smiles at our little brother. "Wanna have 'fun' helping Rachel with that?" He nods toward a wooden bowl of shiny red apples at the other end of the table.

"Sure!" Izzy says.

I shake my head so hard, my braids bounce around. "I am not making charoset."

"But you always make it!" Izzy's eyes are as large as Dylan's matzoh balls.

"Not anymore." I push the bowl away.

Grandma Clara places the wooden bowl between us, and we each grab a peeler and a shiny red apple and get to work.

Making charoset is our specialty. We've been doing it together ever since I was around Izzy's age, when she started flying up from Miami to spend the week of Passover with us here in Maryland.

"Do you think after we finish the charoset, we should peel the celery for the karpas? To get rid of all the yucky stringy parts?" I wrinkle my nose like Izzy.

"Celery . . ." Grandma Clara shakes her head, but her eyes sparkle like always.

There are a million things to love about her, but those blue eyes are one of my favorites. I'm the only grandchild who inherited them. I like to think that's why we see so many things the same way.

"In my day—before electricity . . ." She winks to show she's kidding. "We always dipped parsley in the salt water, not celery."

"What's wrong with celery?"

Grandma Clara shrugs. "Nothing. Except for those yucky stringy parts."

We laugh. "Speaking of celery," I say, "Jordan wants

a vegan Seder Plate this year." He always likes to try new things. I glance at my grandmother, curious to see her reaction.

"Well . . ." She thinks for a few seconds. "I think it's fun to mix things up now and then."

I don't. I like things to stay exactly the same. "Dad says the day he eats from a vegan Seder Plate is the day he makes a ham-and-matzoh sandwich."

"I'm trying to imagine what goes on a vegan Seder Plate," she says.

"I think they use roasted beet for the shank bone, and an avocado pit instead of an egg."

Grandma Clara throws some apple peel into the trash can and considers the idea. "Interesting." She grabs another apple. "What do *you* think of a vegan Seder?"

I love that she asks. With two talkative parents and two very opinionated older brothers, no one ever asks what *I* think about anything. So I take my time before answering. "I think I'd rather have a chocolate Seder."

Grandma Clara's whole face breaks into a huge smile. "So would I." She puts her hand on my shoulder. "Maybe next year."

~~~~~

Now "next year" is here, but there's no chocolate Seder.

All I want is to go back to my room—back to *Little Women*—and be left alone. I'm about to head upstairs when our oldest brother walks into the room. Jordan carefully places the holiday candlesticks and hand-painted Seder Plate on the table.

I love that Seder Plate. I love that Mom and Dad brought it back from Jerusalem and that it came with Elijah's cup and six little bowls. Each bowl has lettering in Hebrew and English that matches the writing on the Seder Plate: egg, horseradish, shank bone . . .

"I'm in charge of the salt water!" Izzy pipes up, happy to be part of it all.

I used to be, too. Jordan looks over in my direction, expecting me to make my usual contribution. Instead, I tell him, "I'll set the table and wash the karpas."

He looks like he's about to say something, then just sits down and starts peeling an apple. I watch him cut off a piece and give it to Izzy, then I head to the fridge.

"Rachel—the celery should be on top," Dylan says.

"I'm not looking for celery." I push aside carrots and onions, broccoli and peppers . . .

"I hope Mrs. Keller's baby shows up soon so Mommy can come home," Izzy says, his mouth full of Honeycrisp. "When's Daddy coming home?"

"He called a little while ago," Jordan says. "His meeting ran long, so he's stuck in rush hour."

I close the vegetable drawer—hard—and open the fruit drawer in case it's there instead. I search through grapes, strawberries, lemons . . . "Why don't we ever have any parsley around here?"

Izzy joins me, his face a question. "What do you need parsley for?"

"To dip in the salt water."

My little brother wrinkles his nose. "We always use celery!"

"I don't want to use celery." My eyes threaten to overflow, but I'm more angry than sad, so I yell instead. "I'm sick of celery!"

"Me too!" Izzy cries out. I doubt he has any strong feelings toward celery, but my little brother is nothing if not loyal.

"And why isn't anybody here?" I ask no one in particular.

"I'm here," Izzy says in a small voice.

And I can't help it any longer. I feel hot tears on my cheeks and his little kid arms around me. I wipe my eyes and ruffle his curls.

"Hey," Dylan says. "We're here, too." He and Jordan join us in front of the fridge. It's kind of crowded, but nice, too. In a corny sort of way.

"Feel like a quick grocery run?" Jordan asks.

"Tell me more about this chocolate Seder." Grandma Clara pours half a cup of grape juice into the shiny metal bowl.

Then it's my turn. I squeeze in some honey and stir it with a wooden spoon, doing my best to coat all the little pieces of apple. "Well, I don't know everything," I admit.

"Mom went to one a couple years ago. The main idea is that freedom is sweet."

"Can't argue with that." She smiles and hands me the cinnamon.

I sprinkle it over the apples and try to remember more. "I think they had four cups of chocolate milk instead of wine . . . And instead of dipping a green vegetable in salt water, they dipped strawberries in chocolate syrup."

"I wonder what they used for bitter herbs."

I think for a few seconds. "Oh—I remember! Bittersweet chocolate."

"Clever."

"My favorite part was the Ten Plagues. I don't remember all of them, but one was cavities and another was indigestion."

Grandma Clara laughs, then hands me a new spoon and waits as I sample the charoset. I give a thumbs-up. "Perfect. As always."

I hand the spoon back to her and she tries it, too. "Mmm. Just right. We make a good team." She covers the bowl in plastic wrap and places it in the fridge.

"So? What do *you* think of the chocolate Seder?" I ask.

She tilts her head to the right the way she does when giving something careful thought. My dad does it, too. "I think . . . I have a sudden craving for something chocolate."

I laugh. "So do I!"

"You know," she says, "we still have a little time before everyone else gets home. And plenty of time before the sun goes down and it's officially Passover."

I'm not sure where she's heading, but I'm happy to follow.

Her blue eyes sparkle even brighter than usual and she leans in close. "It's . . . possible I have a not-kosher-for-Passover item or two in my suitcase."

"Grandma! We were supposed to get rid of all the chametz yesterday!" Every year, we clear the house of all non-Passover foods (mostly things that have flour) before the Seder. Our family always makes it fun by eating whatever pretzels or cookies or cereal we have left before giving the rest away— usually to our non-Jewish friends.

"Guess you'd better help me dispose of it, then . . ."

I don't need to be told twice.

✦✦✦

Jordan and I lock our bikes in the grocery store parking lot and go inside.

"Hey—thanks for doing this," I tell him.

"No problem. I'm always happy to get out of work."

The truth is, everything was almost finished before my mini-meltdown. He's just being a good big brother, so I play along. "Next year, we should let Izzy do all the work."

"Definitely," Jordan says. "Of course, the entire Seder Plate would be filled with candy." He smiles at me.

I try to smile back, but it reminds me of the chocolate Seder and I feel like crying again.

"You OK, Ray?"

I take a breath and nod, then we enter the store and I head straight to the produce section, skipping all the fruit and ending exactly where the parsley is—or should be. Only it's not there. "Are you kidding me? Where's the parsley?"

Jordan moves other green things around on a shelf I can't reach, in case the parsley is playing hide-and-seek or something.

"I can't believe it!" I want to flop down on the floor like when I was little, right there under the cauliflower and asparagus.

Suddenly Jordan shows me a lone bunch of parsley he's managed to unearth from somewhere: the scrawniest, limpest, most pathetic parsley I've ever seen. I honestly don't know if I should cry or laugh.

"Ta-da!" And somehow he manages to say it with a straight face.

※⁂

One of the perks of being the only girl in my family is that Grandma Clara sleeps in my room. It's like a slumber party—for a whole week! She uses my bed and I use a sleeping bag and we stay up way past my bedtime. She talks about what she wanted to be when she was my age, and I talk about what I want to be when I'm her age. Sometimes I show her funny videos on YouTube or teach her a new card game, and some-times she shows me an old dance step.

"You may laugh," she says as she twirls me around the room, "but, someday, knowing how to waltz could come in handy."

One of my favorite things is seeing what she pulls out of her huge red suitcase. Sometimes it's a new book—or an old one that's really special, like *Little Women*. Other times it's a photo album with pictures of her and my dad when they were much younger.

Right now, though, Grandma Clara opens her suitcase and pulls out the contraband chametz: two soon-to-be-forbidden chocolate cupcakes carefully wrapped in plastic.

My mouth waters immediately. "Where did you get those?"

She wiggles her eyebrows, opens the pack, and hands one to me. "Shall we?"

We bite into the moist, fudgy cake at the same time, two very contented chocoholics.

"There's one thing I don't get about the chocolate Seder," I tell her, my mouth still full of cake. "Salt water is supposed to represent the tears of slavery, but chocolate syrup? What does that have to do with tears?"

Grandma Clara tilts her head and thinks. I eat more cupcake and wait patiently; her answers are always worth the wait.

"Well, tears aren't always sad," she says.

"What do you mean?"

"I cried the day I married your grandfather, and he cried when your dad was born. Happy tears on both occasions—the happiest." She covers my hand with hers. "And I seem to recall your father shedding a tear or two when you came along, as well."

"I guess. But that still doesn't work for the Seder Plate."

She looks at me, her blue eyes staring into mine. "What about when the slaves were finally free? What kind of tears do you suppose they cried then?"

"Happy ones."

"You might even call them 'sweet,'" Grandma Clara says.

By the time Jordan and I make it back, both of our parents are home. Mom gives me a kiss and Dad gives me a long, tight hug.

The dining room table is set and it looks beautiful. Our special holiday plates are gleaming, and the brisket in the oven already smells amazing. Izzy places the little blue bowl for salt water next to the Seder Plate: Everything is in place.

It won't be long now before we start this year's Seder.

"Did you get the parsley?" Dylan asks as I reach into the grocery bag.

"Not exactly."

"So what 'exactly' did you get?"

"You'll see."

"Can *I* see?" Izzy jumps up and goes straight for the bag, but I'm too fast for him. "Is it a bagel?" he asks.

"It is! I figured a bagel was the perfect thing for our Seder Plate."

He giggles, and I tickle him, and he giggles some more. "Hey . . ." I bend down so we're eye to eye. "If I tell you what's in the bag, will you keep it a secret?"

He nods so fast his face blurs, and I know he's all in; he always is. I put my head close to his and, as I whisper into his ear, a smile spreads across his face. Then I rinse the surprise ingredient in the sink and put it in the fridge for later.

When the sun sets, our Seder begins. Mom lights the candles, and Dad says the blessing over the first cup of wine (or grape juice), and we all open our haggadahs like we do every year. Only this *isn't* like every year.

This year, my favorite part of Passover is missing.

My parents and brothers are around the table, but it feels empty and lonely and my stomach aches and my heart hurts and I'm missing her so much—

"Izzy?" Dad's voice brings me back. "Could you please pass the salt water?"

Izzy shakes his head. "I can't."

Dad looks baffled. "Why not?" He tilts his head . . . just like Grandma Clara.

"It's a secret!" Izzy announces.

I look at my little brother and he half winks, half blinks at me. I realize we're already at Karpas, the part of the Seder where we dip the green vegetable into salt water. Only not tonight.

I look around the table, hoping everyone will be OK with what I'm about to do. "I know the Four Questions come later, but we all know why *this* night is different from all the others. Why *this* Seder is different from all the others."

Mom reaches for Dad's hand; Jordan stares at his empty plate; Dylan's eyes fill. Izzy looks at me and asks, "Is it time?"

I nod, and we both stand up. "We'll be right back," I tell the rest of our family.

My little brother and I go to the kitchen. He fills a plate and I fill a bowl and we bring them back and place them both on the Seder Plate.

"I've been missing Grandma Clara so much..." My voice cracks.

"Me, too," Dylan says.

"We all have." Mom reaches across the table and covers my hand with hers.

"It's been even worse this week," I say.

"We know." Jordan puts an arm around my shoulder.

Dad sighs. "It's been very hard for all of us."

"Everybody's sad," Izzy says, his face much more serious than usual.

"That's just it," I tell him. "Grandma Clara wouldn't want us to be sad. She'd want us to remember all the fun we had together and how much we loved her." I have to stop for a few seconds, then I take a breath and keep going, like she would want me to. "I think she would say it's OK for us to cry . . . but our tears don't have to be just salty. They can be sweet, too."

I nod at Izzy and he passes the plate of strawberries around the table, and I pass a bowl of salted chocolate caramel sauce and say the blessing.

Everyone answers, "Amen," then we dip the fruit into the chocolate and eat it.

I close my eyes and see Grandma Clara. I see her bright blue eyes, and I see her smile at me.

And I smile back through salty, and sweet, tears.

YACHATZ

Step four: Yachatz. Matzah makes its first appearance but isn't eaten. Not yet. During this step, a matzah is broken in half. One piece is kept at the table while the other is put aside. (In many communities, this piece is hidden for children to search for and find in a later step.) Breaking things is not unheard of among Jewish traditions. At many Jewish weddings, a glass is broken during the ceremony. In many Jewish homes, a small part of the house might remain deliberately unfinished. The world is not perfect; it has broken and missing pieces. And that's OK.

- *The piece of matzah hidden for later is called the afikoman. Is there anything you've ever put aside and saved for later? Is there anything you wish you had? Or wish you hadn't?*

- *The breaking of the matzah is the last step before the story of the Exodus is told. Why do you think that is?*

- *Is there anything in your life that isn't exactly perfect but that you love anyway? That maybe you love in part because it's not perfect?*

- *There is a concept in Judaism called tikkun olam, which means "repairing the world." When you look around, do you see anything that's broken? Do you see anything that you can fix?*

BROKEN PIECES

BY JOSHUA S. LEVY

"Who cares?"

The table went silent. Elisha's parents and siblings. His aunt and uncle. Even his grandfather.

"Elisha!" his mom snapped, drops of her southern accent spilling out, like it always did when she was upset. "Apologize."

Grandpa Nathan held up a hand. "It's all right, Abigail." He turned to the rest of the children around the table. "Who can tell Elisha here why we dip vegetables in salt water?"

Elisha's oldest, perfectest sister, Zara, shot up her hand. Elisha rolled his eyes.

"We dip vegetables in salt water to remember the tears we cried when we were slaves in Egypt!" Zara explained, without anyone calling on her.

"Excellent," Grandpa Nathan said. "Thank you. Next step: Yachatz."

Elisha wasn't satisfied. He had a thousand other things on his mind: history homework, Mr. Simon's science test, whether he was going to get an invite to Gabby Shunem's bat mitzvah. So he picked a bit of parsley from his teeth and tried again. "OK. But, like, *who cares?*"

Grandpa Nathan lowered his haggadah. "I'm going to need you to be more specific."

"Not trying to be rude," Elisha said. "Seriously, who cares? *Why do you care?* I get it. Once upon a time, bad things happened and then we were free. But that was forever ago. That was *then*." Elisha held out his arms at his grandfather's home; at their family, gathered to visit for the holiday; at the entire world. "This is *now*."

Elisha's aunt choked out a cough and took a sip of wine. His parents shifted in their seats. Even Zara stared down at her hands, lost for words for maybe the first time in her life.

"This *is* now, Elisha," Grandpa Nathan answered, without answering. "And we're all hungry. So let's move on. Step four: Yachatz."

Something had changed in the air around the table, but Elisha couldn't tell what. He really wasn't trying to be rude. It was just . . . didn't they have better things to do than tell some confusing old story for five hours—then do it all over again tomorrow night, and twice every year, for all eternity?

Grandpa Nathan held the middle matzah high. They'd sprung for the handmade stuff this year: round matzah as big as the Seder Plate, each piece with charred edges and a bumpy Martian terrain spread across its surface.

"Break the middle matzah," Grandpa narrated from the haggadah.

Crack. Clean in two, each hand clutching a half-moon shard, held apart like a two-piece puzzle about to be solved. And—

That's it. Grandpa Nathan just held the pieces there, arms up, still.

"Grandpa?" Elisha asked, scanning the table for help. But something was wrong. Something *else* had changed in the air.

His mom was looking up at Grandpa Nathan, her mouth stuck halfway toward a smile. His dad was taking a sip of water, but—even with the glass tilted up, water flowing down—nothing poured out. Across the table, Elisha's youngest sister, Beth, had flicked a chunk of charoset high. The little nugget was *stopped in the air above their heads*, like a little sun stood still.

It was as though someone had pressed pause on Elisha's life. Everyone—*everything*—was frozen.

"Mom? Dad?"

No response.

Elisha stood up, tap-tap-tapping his older sister on the shoulder. "Zara?!" Elisha shouted. "I'm smarter than you! Grammar is boring!"

Still nothing. This was bad. "Anyone? Hello?"

Elisha grabbed the dining room landline. No dial tone. He pulled his mom's iPhone out of her purse, swiping and clicking. It was dead, frozen on the lock screen, the time displaying 99:99. Elisha ran back to the table. He didn't know what to do, *if anything could be done.* Where to go, *if there was anywhere to go.*

He stopped next to Grandpa Nathan, matzah still held high. Was there something strange about it? About those jagged edges where the one piece had cracked into two. A color? A glow?

A jumble of panic and curiosity, Elisha held out a finger, touched the larger of the two halves—and rocketed backward.

It all happened in the span of a moment: The matzah glowed red-hot; Elisha was blasted clear over the table; and a crack formed in the middle of the dining room. A crack that seared the air from floor to ceiling. A lightning bolt with edges in the exact pattern as the broken matzah. And then—

Silence, which gave way to a thin, small sound briefly ringing in Elisha's ears before a man stepped through the ripple of light, which sizzled and blinked gone.

Elisha, unhurt, scuttled to his feet. "What . . . ? Who . . . ?"

The man had long hair and a leather belt cinched around sand-colored robes. He strode forward, jutted out his hand, and said, "Caramel?" He unwrapped a little candy and popped it in his mouth before offering another to Elisha.

Too shocked to speak, Elisha shook his head.

The man shrugged and tossed the second caramel in the air. It disappeared into nothing. "Suit yourself. Now then . . ." He looked around the table until his eyes came to rest on a silver goblet in the very center, filled to the top with wine. "Oooh! This for me?" He leaned down to take a sip. "Cabernet? Blech. I liked last year's Pinot better."

"Um, who are you?" Elisha interrupted, finding his voice. "What is going on?"

With a start, the man stood up eerily straight, his brown eyes suddenly white as snow. "I WILL BRING YOU," the man said, his voice a ghostly chorus. It made Elisha's head hurt. Then the man jolted his own head as if to clear it, and—with a kind of exhausted look on his face—said, "Sorry. That happens sometimes. Comes with the gig."

Elisha would have been more afraid, if the stranger didn't suddenly seem so sad.

"And your name?" Elisha asked.

"Huh?"

"Your name. What's your name?"

The man snapped his fingers, and a new plastic-wrapped caramel popped into existence. He plucked it from the air and tossed it into his mouth, wrapper and all. "I've gone by many names over the years. I answer to Elijah, or Eliyahu, or Eli, or Elias, or Pinchas—but he's kinda cranky—or Sandalphon—but he's a bit spooky—or Tishbi, or Gil, or the Troublemaker, or the Great One, or the Best One, or the Best Dressed, or the Most Likely to Succeed, or—"

"OK! Lot of names. Gotcha. What do you want me to call you?"

"Huh. No one's ever asked me that before." The man glanced around the room, landing on a small photograph on the mantle: Elisha's grandparents and their old orange tabby. "What was his name?"

Elisha did a double take. This was not how he was expecting his night to go. "The cat?"

"The cat."

"Kevin."

The man nodded and scratched at his stubbly chin. "Kevin. I like that. Call me Kevin."

"And what is all this, *Kevin*? Why are you here?"

Kevin plucked the matzah from Grandpa Nathan's left hand and started nibbling at the edges. "Why are *you* here?"

Elisha rolled his eyes. He didn't understand any of this. Was it real? A hallucination? Some kind of dream? It didn't matter. He may as well play it out. "You gonna teach me some kind of lesson, is that it? Help me see the true meaning of Yachatz, or whatever?"

Kevin collapsed backward into what was at first empty space, until an armchair raced from the living room to catch him. "I don't really do lessons, kid, if you get me."

"I do not."

In response, Kevin just grinned and snapped his fingers.

※⋙⋙

The first thing Elisha noticed was the heat—ninety degrees, a hundred—carried on a breeze that stabbed at the back of his neck. The light came next, bright and searing. Sunlight. Elisha was outside. He was—

Standing at the top of a hill, facing one end of a small, teardrop-shaped island wedged between two rivers. Elisha looked around. *No, not two rivers.* One river—enormous, infinite. The island temporarily sliced its northward flow like a pebble in a stream.

"Nile River," Kevin said. "Welcome to Egypt. Specifically, the island of Elephantine. Summer of 410. BC, as the kids say."

Heart pounding, Elisha lifted a shaky hand to his forehead, shielding his eyes from the sun. If this was a dream, it was the most vivid dream he'd ever had. At his feet, a dirt path snaked forward and down the hill, where a small village—ancient but intact—thrummed with life. The homes were in the center of the island: mudbrick structures, pressed tightly together, fighting for space on this speck of land barely a thousand feet across. Off to the side but still within the town's walls: a set of temple complexes, each one larger than the next.

"Where are we?" Elisha asked, barely above a whisper.

Kevin rolled his eyes. "I told you, *Elephantine!*"

"No, I mean, like, what about it? *Why* are we here?"

Kevin tsked and poked Elisha on the nose. "That's not the same question, silly."

And before Elisha could try again (or poke Kevin into the Nile River), two teenagers nearly bowled them over. "Look," one said to the other as they rushed past, "I *am* sending you vegetables. Get to the dock tomorrow before the boat comes in on account of Shabbat so they don't spoil. If you don't, I swear . . ."

And then the kids were gone, up the hill, around the bend, out of sight. Elisha did a double take. "There are Jews here?"

Kevin shrugged. "Are, were, will be. That's kind of the whole megillah right there."

"Is this . . ." Elisha tried to put two and two together. " . . . is this Passover? Like, we're in ancient Egypt. Was . . . was that guy Moses?"

Kevin barked out a laugh. "Ha! No, that was Zack. Zechariah. Nice enough kid. Bit of a hothead. I prefer his dad, Nathan. Now that's a guy who puts out decent wine for Passover. Anyway, the destruction of the Jewish temple at Elephantine is long after the whole Exodus business."

Elisha was standing at the summit of an impossibly old Jewish settlement. But the thing Elisha found most unbelievable was that there was someone here with his grandfather's name. He was about to ask if anyone on the island was named "Elisha." But then he remembered something else Kevin had said.

"Destruction?"

Kevin lowered his eyes for a moment. Closed them in a kind of wince. Then he lifted his hand and pointed at the smaller of the two temples: a rectangular shrine in the center of a larger open-air courtyard. The shrine was built with a wooden roof and five stone-lined doorways, each with sparkling bronze hinges. Its entrance faced a square altar, a column of smoke even now reaching into the sky, giving the air the faint smell of burnt toast. Men in white robes busied themselves in the courtyard—pulling animals by the reins, sweeping the floors, washing their hands.

Towering over the whole thing was an even larger temple. Two, three times bigger at least. Gilded and bejeweled, the larger temple surrounded an enormous statue of a half-man, half-sheep. Giant black horns at the top of his head. Knife in one hand.

"The colossal ram idol isn't ours," Kevin pointed out. "Not our speed."

And then they stood by and watched the destruction.

Slowly, methodically, a line of priests made their way out of the Egyptian temple, down a nearby road, and across to the main gates of the Jewish temple courtyard. Joined by a garrison of armed Egyptian soldiers, the mob entered the smaller, unprotected Jewish temple and razed it to the ground. They smashed the pillars of stone. Destroyed the five great doors. They burned it all, pushed people aside, stole anything that wasn't nailed down.

The destruction continued, but Elisha, shaking, couldn't bear to watch anymore. He spun around, turning his back on the now-temple-sized plume of smoke reaching for the sky.

"Why is this happening?" he asked.

"Why does anyone destroy anything?" Kevin asked back. "Prejudice? Ignorance? Fear? Power? 'Let us deal wisely with them.'"

That wasn't much of an answer, so Elisha tried a different question. "Is this the end of Jews in Egypt?"

Kevin moved to stand in front of Elisha. "The *end*?! In 407 BC, the Jews here write to Judea for help. The temple is rebuilt a few years later. And while this little community eventually fades, Egyptian Jewry will grow to be among the most important in our history. Alexandria. Oxyrhynchus. Cairo. Philo. Saadia. Maimonides. Love that guy's lemon cakes, by the way."

Kevin smiled, even while the fire from the destruction reflected in his eyes. "This isn't the end," he said, holding up Grandpa Nathan's half-matzah, whose ridges matched the cliffs beyond the Nile shores. "It's barely the beginning."

"OK . . ." Elisha said. "But I still don't get why you're show-ing me this. Because I said, 'Who cares?' No offense. This is interesting and all. But it's still *literally* ancient history. Exodus from Egypt. Elephantine. It's all the same. *Old.* Forever ago."

Kevin sighed, said "Fine," and snapped his fingers again.

※♦♦♦

"Better?" Kevin asked, holding the matzah out in front of him. He pointed it at yet another ancient cityscape, this time on a hill at the edge of a vast desert. At the closer end, the city began with an army barracks. Walls and guard towers.

Enormous flags stitched with ships and bulls. *Thousands* of armored men—red shields in hand, metal plating from head to waist—marched in formation, practice-fighting with swords and spears.

Beyond the military camp lay the city proper: neat blocks of long, column-lined roads; homes and larger buildings, most topped with meticulous rows of clay tiles; statues everywhere. At the edge of the city, overlooking a heap of ruins and a massive stone wall, lay another temple. Familiar to Elisha somehow, in a social-studies-textbook sort of way, like how he knew Egyptian hieroglyphics when he saw them.

Another titanic statue stood at the heart of this temple, atop a towering column of stone. The figure had long hair, a curly beard, and a sheet of bronze draped over muscular shoulders. Lightning bolt held high.

Elisha may not have paid the most attention in social studies. But he *had* read all the Percy Jackson books.

"Is that Zeus?" he asked.

"Poh-tay-toh, poh-tah-toh," Kevin replied. "But the Romans called him Jupiter."

"Wait, are we in *Rome*?!"

Kevin sighed. "Jerusalem, actually. Or it was." He tilted the half-matzah this way and that, like a boat rocking in a stormy sea. "Will be again. A wheel turns around in the world." Kevin's eyes went glassy. "They razed it to the ground during the First Roman-Jewish War back in 70 AD. And Hadrian's grudge from the Kitos War back in 115 eventually led him to rebuild Jerusalem into a mini-Rome. He named the new city after himself—classic—and erected that statue to Jupiter, right where the Second Temple stood, just to stick it to us."

Kevin was rambling now, speaking faster and faster. Elisha wasn't paying much attention. Not to Kevin, at least. "What's that sound?" Elisha asked.

Kevin ignored him. "Hadrian building Aelia Capitolina where Jerusalem had stood—and then forbidding Jews from entering their own city—sparked the *Third* Roman-Jewish War. The Bar Kochba revolt. Doomed from the start."

"What's that sound?" Elisha asked again, trying to focus on the rising cacophony somewhere nearby. There was shouting. Crying. The clapping of horse hooves on cobblestone.

"Did you know that Hadrian is considered one of the 'Five Good Emperors'?" Kevin went on. "The 'Most Excellent' Emperor? One of the best—if not *the* best—there ever was? Except for that one pesky time he killed half-a-million Jews, enslaved countless others, and razed a thousand towns to the ground."

A chariot burst into view, horses galloping up a nearby ridge, an armored rider lashing at the reigns. The horses were pulling a sealed carriage, windows spliced with iron bars. There was a man inside. An old man. A prisoner. As the chariot raced across the horizon, Elisha caught a glimpse of shackles binding the man's wrists.

"Who—?" Elisha started.

But a crowd of people answered before the question was fully asked. "Akiva!" they shouted. Adults and children. At least two dozen of them. Running in the chariot's wake. Following it as fast as their legs could take them, falling behind, not giving up. "Akiva!"

"A good man," Kevin said. "Flawed, but good. Always capable of change. He taught Torah after the Romans outlawed it. Encouraged Bar Kochba against his better judgment."

"What's happening to him?" Elisha asked.

"Captured by the Romans. He's being brought to the legate in Caesarea, who will soon sentence Akiva to death."

More death. More destruction. And then—

A shriek from the crowd. A woman doubled over, hand on her round belly. "Are you all right?" a man standing next to her asked.

"The baby," she said. "Shimon, I think the baby might be near."

"The same year Akiva dies," Kevin whispers, "Yehuda Ha-Nasi is born. Maybe the same *day*. Yehuda will ultimately compile the Mishnah, a text upon which the next millennia of Jewish history will be built. They destroyed a city. We wrote a book. One extraordinary story ends, another begins."

Elisha turned his back on the crowd. They had all stopped chasing Akiva's chariot and instead began to care for the pregnant woman, holding her up, handing her water, gathering a bit of straw for her to lie down.

"I think I get what you're trying to do," Elisha said. "But this doesn't change anything. It's still more ancient history."

Kevin groaned. "But this *isn't* ancient! It's the Pax Romana, baby. The 'Roman peace.' A pretty ironic term, if you ask me. But nobody ever asks me. Except when they do. But then they're impossible questions. Point is, we're in AD now. It's all practically postmodern. I can take you forward *another* five hundred years if you want. But the story here is gonna be about the same."

"I'm sorry." Elisha crossed his arms. "But this is still forever ago. If you're trying to say that Passover isn't just about remembering the Exodus, well, I still don't get why I'm supposed to care about something that happened over a thousand years ago."

Kevin just looked at Elisha. Said, "Kids today." And snapped his fingers again.

※※※

"Welcome to 1862," Kevin said, holding out a hand. "Ulysses S. Grant issues an order expelling all Jews from Tennessee, Mississippi, and Kentucky. This *now* enough for you? Please don't make me take you into the twentieth century. *Please.* There's only so much I can handle."

Ahead, another army camp buzzed with activity. Union flags quivered in the breeze. The evening chill stung Elisha's skin. He was *in* Tennessee. I mean, maybe not *now*. Elisha wasn't sure where he was *now*. But Passover. The table. His grandfather's house in Memphis. They visited from Connecticut every year.

"It didn't work," Elisha said, half a question. "Grant's order. It didn't work."

Kevin smiled. "No. President Lincoln eventually rescinded the order, but not before at least some families were evicted from their homes."

A foghorn rang out. In the distance, a boat chugged along a river even wider than the Nile. Smokestacks breathed their ash into the winter night. Parents held their children close along the bannisters. Candles twinkled on the deck.

Elisha spotted a boy his own age. Hair his own hair. Eyes his own eyes.

"But they'll be back," Kevin continued. "Slavery and freedom. Destruction and rebuilding. Endings and beginnings. For us, for others."

Elisha nodded, his mind swirling with what was, what could have been. He could still see Kevin's words in his eyes: *Please don't make me take you into the twentieth century.*

"OK," Elisha said. "OK."

And Kevin snapped his fingers one last time.

✤

They were back in Grandpa Nathan's house, Elisha's family still frozen in place. For the first time, Elisha noticed a newspaper spread open on the living room coffee table.

Images he didn't understand—of things smashed, destroyed, burned.

Words he didn't want to read—a plume of smoke reaching for the sky.

Something had *happened*. It had happened *here* and it had happened *now*.

Kevin stepped toward Grandpa Nathan and replaced the half-matzah in his hand. Elisha looked around again, at the house, his family, the world. They'd built all this on top of everything that had been destroyed before. Love in here, even after hate out there.

"Is *this* the end of something?" Elisha asked, his voice as cracked as the matzah. "Is it just the beginning?"

Kevin—Elijah, Tishbi, whoever he was—took a step forward and knelt down in front of the boy. "Always with the impossible questions," he said, and then he disappeared.

"Break the middle matzah in two," Grandpa Nathan said again, as the room came back to life.

"Wait," Elisha said, sitting up straight. He was in his chair, breathless, returned to reality. "Grandpa, wait."

Everyone looked to Elisha, who cleared his throat. He didn't know how to start the conversation, but he knew that the conversation had already been started, had never really ended, maybe never would. "The story isn't about forever ago." He shook his head, clenched his eyes shut and opened them again. "I mean it *is*, but it's also about *always*. And *today*. We care because the story is still being told."

Grandpa Nathan smiled. The same smile Elisha had seen on Kevin's face. "We sit around tables and invite others to share with us," Grandpa Nathan said. "We tell stories and laugh. We hope and remember."

Elisha understood. "We dip vegetables in salt water. We break matzahs in half."

His grandfather nodded. "Exactly."

MAGID

Magid. Step five. Retelling the story of Jews achieving their free-dom from Egypt. But the story is not told as you'd expect. And sometimes, it barely feels like a story at all. Magid begins with a description of matzah. It continues with the Four Questions and a short tale of rabbis in the Roman era discussing the Exodus for so long, they lose track of time. There's a story of a family with four children, not all of whom want to be at the Seder. A list of the Ten Plagues (and a ritual where wine or grape juice is spilled, to acknowledge the suffering of others, even those who wished us harm). A bit of thanks. And somewhere in there, the Exodus story, told in pieces: The Jews were enslaved by the Pharaoh. After the Ten Plagues were sent against Egypt, the Pharaoh relented and let them go.

- "Why is this night different from all other nights?" the Four Questions begin. Can you think of a special day or night from your own life? Can you think of at least four things that made it special?

- Magid lists the Ten Plagues brought on Egypt before the Jews were freed. Have you ever lived through a kind of plague? Has anyone in your family? How have things changed? How have they stayed the same?

- One of the most popular songs of the Seder is called "Dayenu." Also contained in the Magid step, the song is about being grateful—how we should appreciate every gift and not always be looking for the next one. Do you think you have enough? What would you be willing to lose? What wouldn't you be willing to lose?

- The Jewish slaves wanted to leave Egypt. But—for a long time—Egypt had also been their home. Have you ever wanted to leave a place, even if a part of you wanted to stay?

NACHSHON IN THE DESERT, ALONE AT THE SEA

BY LAUREL SNYDER

It was the rosefinch's fault, not mine! I'd tried so hard not to stray, kept close to Mother and Elisheva in the crowd, trudging through the sand for days. But when that rosefinch—a flash of pink above me—pierced the sky with her high sharp song, I had to follow. My need to wander matched the flutter in her wings, and so I slipped off for a minute. A minute! Only, the people around me kept moving forward, and somehow, when I glanced back for Mother, I found myself alone in the crowd.

This was nothing new. I was often alone in a crowd. But in that vast desert, the aloneness swallowed me, and I panicked, searched the throng, the jostling calling shuffling bodies around me. I shouted and shouted, but nobody answered. Only some other boy about my age stuck out his tongue. At last I took a deep brave breath, and I walked. Until my belly rumbled and my forehead burned. Until the sun was over there. Until my sandal gave out, and I felt the faint snap of worn leather stretching to its breaking point, and I tumbled into the hot sand, surrounded by dusty feet.

I wasn't sure what to do, and I lay like that awhile, staring up at the fierce sun, while all above and around me, the crowd shifted and moved. It split around my body the way a river splits around a rock. Most of the people barely glanced down at me. "I could stay here," I thought to myself. "I could go to sleep right here in the sand, and no one would even care." Briefly, I closed my eyes.

But they'd keep coming, I knew, thousands of them. A herd of feet trampling past. A city on the march, and if they didn't pummel me, I'd fall even farther behind. *Then* how would I find my family when we got to wherever it was we were going? So I pushed myself to standing, shouldered my bag, and trudged forward again, torn sandal in hand, through the bleating goats and grunting cattle, the babies whining and wailing. Other kids ran past me, playing with sticks or chasing each other, somehow laughing in the heat. But they didn't ask me to join them, and I marched forward, wincing each time the bare sole of my right foot touched the blazing desert floor.

We'd been walking for days by that point, the whole world of us—on water rations and the dry husks we'd been told to call matza. The meat had run out. The oil, too. None of us had ever been so far from home, and none of us knew where we were going. There were rumors, of course, and I overheard them at night, when we made camp and I took my solitary walks. Families gathered around campfires to swap tales.

Someone had it from someone who had it from someone who had it from Moses. But I hadn't seen Moses all week, and as far as I could tell, it was his fault we were here. Life had been hard in Mitzrayim, but at least I'd had fresh bread to eat and my cozy pallet in the corner. What good would Moses do me? Moses commanded and the people followed. Look where it had gotten us.

Still, I walked with them, his followers—those people who had no interest in me—moving slowly on my poor scalded heel. Then the blister broke open and the sand worked its way into the wound, so no matter how I tried to speed up, I only fell farther behind. Hobbling in pain, I was lost in a sea of faces I recognized but didn't know. Would I ever find Mother and Elisheva? I was too old to cry, I told myself, but tears stood in my eyes.

Walking *toward* something, you think about where you're going. Walking *away*, you think about what you've left behind. All that long day, staring at sweaty faces and the blank sky overhead, I couldn't help thinking about home. I remembered the long grasses waving along the banks of the Nile, blue in the shadows at dusk. I thought of sun-warmed figs, stolen from Pharaoh's groves. Would there be figs where we were going? I licked my dry lips and felt my spit thick and pasty on my tongue. When I reached for my water skin and found it empty, I groaned. The well at home was sweet and cold, even if it had never belonged to us.

I felt lost in it, my hunger for home. Why were we here? What were we doing, heading out into the distance? What kept us on this terrible march? If I'd never been exactly happy at home, I'd never felt an aching fear inside me. If I'd never fit in, I'd never been *this* alone.

That night, I slept by myself in the sand, among the unfamiliar snoring and wheezing and breathing bodies, my head on my lumpy sack. Lost in the desert, too parched to sleep, all I had was that bundle and my worries. My foot burned and itched, and I tossed all night, and people around me grunted and called out, "Be still!" and "Silence!" But stillness is not a gift I have, and my mind was as full as my belly was empty.

The next day was more of the same. I woke in the cold desert morning to watch the sunrise bloom overhead. Then I wrapped my foot as well as I could in a piece of cloth torn from my tunic, tied it with the broken sandal strap. After that, all there was to do was walk again, through the crowd, if never quite with it. I begged sips of water from other people's mothers, tried to ignore the rumblings in my belly.

Until . . . all at once, we stopped moving. Nobody around me seemed to know why, but the march ended. We stalled. Off in the distance, wherever they were, I wondered if my family knew what was happening, if *they* could see what lay ahead of us. But wondering did me no good, and so we all waited, as the moments stretched and stretched. How much time was passing? It was hard to tell how slowly the sun was moving, with no trees or towers to measure it by. As the minutes passed, people began to mutter. "What's the hold up?" they fussed. "Where's Moses?" Everywhere, people looked uneasy, shifted from foot to foot, shot one another frightened glances, but nobody did anything. There was only a stirring, a rustling. Everyone happy to grumble, unwilling to move.

But when people began to sit, tiredly, in the sand around me, to flop to the ground, sighing as they leaned against one another, I found I could not stand it. How could *this* be a time for sitting still? I watched a man scratch his hairy armpit and yawn and found I had to turn away.

Until, above me, I heard a whistle, a sharp song. I glanced up and found my rosefinch had followed us! She darted about freely in the sun's glare and seemed to call to me. And then it was as if something broke in me, as if the waiting shattered, so that I couldn't be still any longer. I couldn't stand to sit like the others. I couldn't settle myself. The journey *couldn't* be over yet, because we hadn't arrived anywhere. Had we? I was still alone. Still starving. My throat was parched. This couldn't be the end.

But how do you know when you're done with a journey?

My eyes on the rosefinch flitting above, I shouldered my bag once more and stepped forward, to move alone. Carefully, I inched my way, nudged the people around me, pushed at them so that they stepped aside. I walked and pushed and walked and pushed against the bodies of strangers. I stepped over those who sprawled on the ground. They seemed so tired, nearly finished. A woman holding a baby looked up at me from where she sat on the ground but said nothing. I made my way through a cluster of skittish goats. I shoved past a group of men, huddled and whispering. I don't know how long I did this, how many hours I spent inching my way forward through the sweaty crowd, skirting body after body, which seemed to be packed closer and closer together the farther I got to the front.

What was I looking for, I wondered? My family, but not only that. I wasn't certain why I walked, only that I could no longer wait. Better to be on my own and moving. Better to be doing *something*. I looked for the rosefinch, but she was nowhere to be seen.

Meanwhile, the sun sank in the sky. The desert began to cool. And it was nearly dusk when I arrived, when I finally shoved my way to the very front of the march and reached the place I hadn't known I was headed. When I came to the water.

The water!

In front of me, all I could see was water. Stretching into forever. I had never seen so much water before in my life. This was no river or stream. Was it the end of the world? Waves lapped the sand at my feet gently, but beyond that, they grew wild, choppy, and harsh, as the wind blew rough over the water. There was no land in sight, nothing in the distance but more distance.

I stared. I'd never seen anything like it before, and I couldn't have imagined it if I hadn't seen it for myself. In that moment, a new thought woke inside me, and I began to understand. The world was *full* of things I had never seen or imagined, but that didn't mean they weren't there. *Everything* was out there. The whole world was vast and waiting. That was our journey. We were marching to *all* the things I had never imagined. I stared, hungry, in their direction.

Then someone bumped me from behind, and I glanced back, over my shoulder, remembered the crowd. I could see only people, bodies forming another kind of endless sea. My eyes blurred for a moment, with sweat maybe, and it seemed to me that I couldn't make out their individual faces anymore, only a mass in motion, a wave of sounds and eyes. Choppy and moving just like the waves, rippling with murmurs and faint cries. I stood there on the beach between the water and the herd. Moments later, voices began to shout.

"But where shall we go?"

"What will happen now?"

"I haven't eaten in two nights . . ."

"Why did we ever come here?"

A woman screamed without words and then, far off in the distance, we heard it, a great sound that shattered the moment, that changed everything. It was the blast of a horn, familiar and terrible, a shrieking command. My stomach turned as the crowd at my back—that entire city of people, crammed body to body, shoulder to shoulder—fell silent and craned its many heads to look in the direction from which we'd come, back to what had felt like home. We knew the sound too well, that angry blast. Mitzrayim had arrived! Soldiers, with their chariots and swords. Pharaoh, come for us. Somewhere above our heads, an arrow whistled through the sky, pierced the dusk, and landed in the waves beyond.

"Moses?" a voice shouted from a few feet away.

And then another voice. "Moses!"

Soon they all cried, as one. "Moses! Moses!"

All around me, the people were shouting. But where was Moses?

That was when the crowd began to fracture, to break. Now moving not as one creature but as many terrified beasts.

"I'm going back!" shouted a woman, clutching her little boy by the hand. "If they'll have me. I just want to go home."

"No!" shouted a man beside her, grabbing her shoulder. "Fight, I say fight! We outnumber them. We only need to stand firm, sister!"

Elsewhere, people dropped to their knees to pray. Mumbling and stammering all the best words they knew. "Oh God oh God," they sang. "Help us."

And there was crying.

So much crying.

Wailing from every corner.

The voices rose from the sand and met the sunset as it washed the heavens. And I heard them, but it was as if they were a dream of something I'd recently left behind. In front of me was the sea. The unimaginable. In front of me was the beginning of everything else. It was worth the march, to have seen it. To know it was out there. To believe in it now.

And that was when I spotted him at last. Standing high on an outcropping of rock. *There* he was, staff in hand.

And somehow, in that moment, I found my voice. "Moses!" I called.

But Moses didn't glance down. He couldn't hear or he wasn't listening. Only talking. To something else I couldn't see or imagine. Somewhere out *there*, over the water, above us all. Something in the pink and orange ribbons of the sky, the dusky clouds. Moses looked to be pleading with the clouds. He frowned at them, called, gestured with his staff, cajoled.

"MOSES!" I called again, as loudly as I could. "What comes next?"

Then he seemed to hear me. He turned and held out his arms to all of us below. "God will save you," called Moses. "God is with us. God is here."

"When?" I shouted. "Now?"

Moses didn't answer. He turned back around then, to argue with the sky. With his free hand, he reached up and made a motion, as if cupping a breeze, as if gathering something to him.

"WHEN?" I shouted again, louder, so that my voice went shrill. The crowd was pushing against me now, shoving me toward the water, packing more tightly together.

Other cries followed mine. "When? Yes, *when*?" And the cries were fearful, though I felt strangely calm. Despite the cries and arrows, despite the sea and the crowd, I found I was only eager. It was as if I could taste something bright on my tongue. A new kind of hunger, for fruits I'd never seen.

But Moses had no answer for any of us. And all around me, the people began to shout again. "Doom!" cried a man. "He's led us nowhere. It's the end!"

"But . . ." I whispered to myself, as I was pushed from behind and stumbled forward again, the sand suddenly damp underfoot. "But this can't be the end. When it feels so much like the beginning." I stared out at that vast, beautiful water.

The sand was cooler here. It felt good on my poor foot. When I closed my eyes, it was as if time took a slow breath. As if all the voices blended into one voice for a moment, as if their bodies disappeared, and I was by myself on the beach, with foam at my feet. Just me. Alone by the water.

I opened my eyes then, to stare at the sea again, and it felt . . . *good*. Perhaps we were trapped, but even so, everything was beautiful. And look! I could still close my eyes, or open them. I could let out a deep breath, or hold it. My feet were my own, however sore they might be. Nothing could be over while I was still moving, breathing, thinking such thoughts. I gazed out at the water.

Then I looked beyond it. I strained to look past it, into the distance, where the water met the sky. "What *else* is there?" I asked myself. "What else can't I imagine?"

And that was when, above me, I heard a familiar sound: a song. My rosefinch!

I stared up at her. "Do *you* know what's out there?" I asked. I shouted up at the sky. "Do you know how far it is? Do you know where we're going?"

She only hovered, silent, but as if in answer, a wave reached up then, to lap at my toes. I startled at that, peered down, and wondered.

"How far *is* it?" I asked the ocean.

It only lapped a little farther, up onto my foot. A strange invitation.

And then I knew.

I knew when.

I knew how.

Or anyway, I believed I did.

Gently, I stepped into the shallows of that great blue sea. I couldn't swim, but somehow that didn't stop me. Forward was the only direction left, and so I would go there. Into the world I couldn't see or imagine. It was cool, the sea. It felt good on my torn foot.

I walked in, up to my ankles, and nobody noticed.

I walked in, up to my knees.

I walked farther.

When the cold water hit the soft skin of my belly, a shudder went down my spine, and the hairs on my arms stood up. I sucked in a quick breath, turned to glance behind me. People had noticed now. People were staring, and silent. But nobody followed. I peered up at the rocks above the beach and found that even Moses was staring. His staff had fallen low, to his side. He gazed down.

I stepped in deeper, up to my chest. I laughed. Water splashed my shoulders, and I felt split in two by the blazing sun on my face and the chilly depths that held my body. With my eyes on Moses, I took one more step and fell under the surface. As I did, I stretched my arms wide to welcome the sea. And as the waves pulled me down, the last thing I saw was Moses's staff, suddenly aloft, raised to that beautiful sky, the dusk settling.

Under the water, eyes squeezed tight against the sting of salt, I could see nothing, could only *feel*. The sand beneath my feet, full of stones and pebbles. The eddies curling and whipping against my skin, pulling my tunic with it, so that it floated up around my chest. The faint glimmer of a fish against my back. The tremor of the current. But more than anything, I felt my breath, waiting.

Lost in the unimaginable, I counted the moments. And it was then, when I could stand it no longer, when the last great gasp of air I'd taken would wait no longer to leave my body . . . that I opened my mouth and found . . . a breeze! The miracle of shifting tides and my own good breath. I was *not* drinking the sea. But gasping. Panting. Eyes still squinted against the salt water in them, I sputtered and gulped the wind, as I looked around and saw the waves.

The waves! The waves were falling away, sinking quickly, disappearing around my very body. By the time I shook the water from my hair, the sea was gone, disappeared from around my shoulders, torso, even from beneath my feet. The sea had somehow split in two and rearranged itself, so that it now towered above us, cliffs of water on either side. I stared around, gazed at the strange walls of water.

"Look!" I cried to the people. "Look!"

But nobody answered. They were already running, all of them. They were moving forward now, together. Everyone dashing as quickly as they could across the muddy bed where the sea had been.

And though I had been at the front of the herd only a moment before, I hung back, stood a while before I joined them. Still panting, breathing hard. I tugged my wet tunic back into place and glanced around at the people sprinting, the people who had stood so long that day. They splashed the mud, but nobody seemed to mind; they were grasping hands and calling to each other. All around us, there was shouting. Shouting everywhere!

When I heard a familiar voice call my name, I turned toward my sister. "Elisheva!" I cried.

"Nachshon!" She ran to me with wide eyes. She reached out to hug me. "Where have you been? We were so frightened when you went missing! Mother's been weeping since you disappeared."

Caught in her relieved embrace, I peered up then, at Moses, on his rock. He still held his staff out, extended over the now-dry seabed, but his eyes were not on it. Instead, he stared down at me with an odd expression. I wasn't sure what to make of it. I didn't know exactly what his eyes were saying. But they looked . . . pleased.

Elisheva caught none of that. "Come," she said, when she released me. "We need to move on, before the sea returns."

"All right," I said. "All right. Of course. I'll come."

But I didn't follow her right away. I held back, because at that moment, I heard a song above me, a shrill call. And when I looked up, I found my rosefinch waiting.

"Thank you!" I called out.

"Strange boy!" Elisheva shouted at me, laughing. "Always off, wandering alone. That'll do you no good. Come and join the rest of us."

So I laughed, too.

And as the rosefinch flew off, my sister grabbed my hand and pulled me forward, into the crowd, across the sea, to wherever our story was taking us. As the sun set, I let her. I followed Elisheva and the rest of them, into the darkness and whatever came next.

RACHTZAH

Step six is called Rachtzah. Hands are washed again, followed by the recital of a short blessing, "Al Netilat Yadayim." There is also a practice of remaining silent between this step and the next, when the matzah is eaten. The quiet between steps represents the connection between them. A lack of interruption. We're so excited to finally eat the matzah that we can't even speak.

- *Of all the actions to repeat, why do you think handwashing is repeated—in step two and here?*

- *Maybe you've reread a book, rewatched a movie, practiced a skill over and over. What happens when you repeat something? How is the experience changed?*

- *The "Al Netilat Yadayim" blessing is not just said on Passover. Many Jews wash their hands and say these words every time they eat bread (unleavened and regular) throughout the year. While the "Urchatz" washing step is unique to this holiday, the "Rachtzah" washing step is not. If you could create your own holiday—remixing brand-new rituals with others borrowed from throughout the year—what would that holiday be for, and how would you celebrate?*

- *What is the loudest silence you have ever heard?*

THE GREAT HANDWASHING MACHINE

BY CHRIS BARON

I NEVER
want to wash
my hands again
  even though I'm known
  to let myself get messy.
  My mom says that's OK
  because inventors
  need to get their hands
  into all kinds of things.
At school,
we wash all the time,
before Robotics lab
and after coding class.
At Hebrew school, they teach us to wash even more;
  when we wake up
    before we eat
    after we eat
      after we go to the bathroom.
We wash until our fingers shrivel into frayed wires.

GRANDPA ZEV

That's why I couldn't believe it
when Grandpa Zev,
in his booming voice
while giving all of us
roles for the Passover Seder
declared, *Eli, this year you will be
in charge of Rachtzah,
handwashing before the meal!*

In all of Passover
there is nothing
    more sacred
        more scary
            more important
                than *any* job
                    Grandpa Zev asks us to do.

I didn't realize he'd even asked me
until I felt the weight of his hands
on my shoulder,
his fingers, blocks of iron,
his wary eyes like empty lanterns
waiting to be lit by my answer.
    Maybe he gave me this job
        because he remembers
           I like the quiet parts

                    of the Seder the best,

                        or because the job is simple

and he thinks I'm too
young to understand
the deeper meaning?
Or maybe it's because
Grandpa Zev is an inventor
just like me, and he wants
me to do something great!

But Grandpa Zev
is hard to impress.
I know he loves me, but usually,
when I show him my inventions,
like the fly-swatting tennis racket,
or the "Kosher for Passover" potato battery
that electrocuted his long beard,
he says, "Hmm, I like it,

                but keep trying."
Maybe this is my chance
to make him proud.

                He waited on my answer.

                    I said nothing and nodded. So did he.

GRANDMA MAE

Grandpa Zev doesn't like
when things change.
That's why this Seder
is especially hard.

It's the first
since he started having trouble
remembering.

Grandma Mae
tries to make up for his silence,
his frustration,
has plates
of macaroons
when we come
through the door,
tells us stories
about farms in faraway places.

At the Seder,
they are the ones
who make it real,
show us photos
of the ships
like the one
they took to America,
make us feel

like the stories
are as alive as a
fig tree in full bloom,
budding with life.

But since things changed,
it seems like Grandpa Zev's
stories have all run out.
His words seem a little hollow,
like a robot
          with his batteries
                    running low.

TRADITIONS

Even though he's a little lost right now,
Grandpa Zev still believes in traditions
and rules and things that never change.

          This Seder is important,
          and so is this job,
          because even though
          my inventions don't always work,
          they have the power to make him smile.
                    I hope.

Maybe this is my chance
to find him again,
to impress him,
help him remember.

> I spend the week before
> building the perfect machine.
> I can't mess this up.

BEFORE THE SEDER

My cousins arrive
from all around town,
gather in my room.
I'm glad they are here
even though it gets loud
when they are.
I like it when things are quiet.
It's easier to think, to invent.
Sometimes they say
I'm too quiet,
but I like to speak
with the things I make.

We work on our parts for the Seder,
helping to tell the story:
> Parting the Red Sea,

plague artwork,

building matzah houses,

making songs out of the questions,

finding the Afikomen.

Nathan folds one thousand paper frogs

even though he is distracted

by my balloon-powered race car

I built with Legos and string.

Andrew reads about the Red Sea,

wraps duct tape around an old hockey stick,

turning it into a staff.

Little Yael, on her third lollipop,

her lips turned red and blue,

tosses my egg-drop container

up and down while she

memorizes questions.

Stacy sits in the corner reading,

motionless, a new teenager

caught between the adults,

twelve-year-old me,

and the younger cousins.

She sees my machine in the corner,

all tubes and wires balancing

on a shiny, wheeled, kitchen cart.

What will THIS thing do? She asks.

I've built the perfect machine, I say.

It's a real Rube Goldberg. It's for Rachtzah.

She rolls her eyes. *Great,* she says. *Anything to make the
Seder go faster.*

I inspect the machine,
count ball bearings,
push and **P u ll**—on levers and string.

Cool! Nathan says, running over.

Can I try? Yael appears like she teleported.

Careful I warn them, but their hands are already
pushing and pulling every component.

How will this wash our hands? Andrew asks.

Does it work? It's so heavy, says Nathan,
trying to lift the water jug.

We'll see, I say, proudly. *And remember,*
after each person washes, they get quiet
until we are all quiet
until everyone's done.
I'll go last
and then we can eat.

Can you do it fast? asks Yael. *I'm hungry already,*
and takes a toothy bite of her blue lollipop.

Nothing is fast during Passover, Stacy groans.

*Especially since Grandpa Zev has to hear things twice
sometimes.*

With the mention of his name

the energy f i Z Z l e s out
and questions stop.
Yael walks over to me,
her eyes suddenly wet,
looks up with blue lips.
I smile, put her hand
on the box of matzah
that activates the whole thing.
I whisper to her, *I hope it works*.

WHAT IT MEANS

I make a few more adjustments:
      flex the tubing,
      inspect the five-gallon water jug,
      tighten the plastic spigot,
      which seems a little loose.

I imagine it working perfectly,
the first lever activating,
each part doing its job
so the water flows
      three   perfect   times.
Then Grandpa Zev
will give a smile,
happy again
like the old him,

proud of me at last
like I finally understand
what the Seder is about.

        I don't always understand what it's about.

He once told me,
after next year,
after my bar mitzvah,
that I will start to see
a different meaning.
All the elements of the Seder
will look different,
the juice will turn to wine,
the maror more bitter,
the matzah more dry.
The river of words
won't drown me anymore,
and the drumbeat prayers
banging over and over
will suddenly make sense,
sinking into the deepest parts of me.

Cousin Stacy says it's "kinda true"
                it *will* mean more.

For me, it's the quiet moments
at the Seder that mean the most,
and even though I'm sick of it,
I am a handwashing expert.
In the great machine of Passover,
it's the simplest component.
It just means "to wash."

After the story and the songs,
but just before the matzah
that tells us it's time to eat,
we have Rachtzah,
where we wash our hands
a second time,
and the best part is
the quiet until,
one by one,
everyone is finished.
Everyone will get to see my machine,
and since I'm the last to wash,
nobody can talk
until *I* wash *my* hands—
only silly noises are allowed,
or the sound of our rumbling stomachs
until we say the Hamotzi blessing
eating the matzah all together.

DISCONNECTED

Grandpa Zev says
Rachtzah is beautiful.

> *Before the meal*
>> *we wash deeply, in silence*
> *after the story of Pesach*
>> *pressing ourselves into the spiritual.*

Grandma Mae adds,

>> *to find a closer connection with each other.*

I'm not sure what the spiritual part means,
but I know the silence is increasing
now that his memories come and go
and he hasn't said much at all this year.
Maybe the Seder and my Rachtzah part
will help with finding a closer connection
because now, everything feels disconnected
like all the circuits in our family are fried.

DEEP INTO THE SEDER

It's different tonight.
On other nights,
on other Seders,
the grown-ups
are loud,
their hands turning our heads
to listen to the words,

telling us to "open our hearts"
and relive the stories.
>A story machine with all the parts
>whizzing and whirring together.

But on this night
everyone seems   different,
circuits malfunctioning
like the portions of the Seder
don't fit together
to make the machine run right—
like even one broken piece
can ruin the whole machine.

Aunt Edie looks
at the food in the kitchen,
shakes her head
like we forgot something.
My father quietly stares
into the saltwater bowl
like he's trying
to move it with his mind.
Uncle Paul smiles,
slides his phone
back into his pants pocket.

Grandpa Zev grasps the haggadah
with giant fingers,
    his low breath
        slightly fluttering
            the corner of the pages.
Usually he would notice
every distraction,
swallow it all
with a word and a look
like our ancestors come to life.
This year he misses everything—
even Yael poking Nathan under the table.
Grandma Mae loops her arm in his,
and he smiles in sudden memory and place.

But even though
the family machine
feels disconnected,
each of us does our job
    dipping,
        breaking,
            and finally reciting.
We know that this means
the food is coming soon
and just before that
it will be time for

The Great Hand-Washing Machine
but first we finish
telling the story.

PLAGUES

Even though the plagues
aren't supposed to be funny,
we laugh because
it feels strange
to dip our fingers
into our cups
and drip onto our plates.
Cousin Nathan
holds his bucket full
of folded paper frogs,
waits for the right moment,
his legs shaking the table
until the moment we chant
FROGS!   Frogs
We reach into the bucket frogs   frogs
tossing paper frogs into the air   frogs
       frogs   frogs frogs
      frogs
  frogs   frogs   frogs
      frogs
watching them fall

like green snow
over the Seder Plates
and wine cups,
into glasses
and salty water.
Grandpa Zev doesn't seem to notice.

THE RED SEA

It's Cousin Andrew's job
to tell the part of the story
where the Israelites
cross the Red Sea.
Find anything that holds water!
He shouts,   pointing to the kitchen cabinets.
                    One by one we fill cooking pots,
                    bowls and pitchers with water,
                    placing them between the
                    table and the kitchen.
These are the Red Sea, he announces
in his deepest voice,
everyone line up at the shore
past the pots and bowls.

But the grown-ups don't   or   won't—
my father decides
to go to the bathroom,

Uncle Paul says,
        I'll watch from my seat
his eyes fixed on his phone.
Grandpa Zev
        lifts his eyes
                just enough to see
                        without really looking.
                                All of them part of the broken
                                machine.

Only my mom gets up.

Andrew hands her the hockey staff of Moses,
the orange tape peeling off.
She sighs, looks at everyone,
then into Andrew's expectant eyes.
Slowly she lifts the staff.
In the quiet   pause
                        the kids take a deep breath.

        Yael and Nathan whisper, *Whoa!*

All of us wondering, just for a moment,
if the water in the bowls might suddenly
swirl into a   VORTEX.

My mom lets out a long exhale
with mystery prayers on her lips,
holding the staff above the water,
the smell of brisket and candles
wafting through the kitchen . . .

Nothing happens.

The water stays still.

Yael groans,
and we let out a sad breath
that comes when a thing
you hoped for doesn't quite happen.

Wait! My mom shouts.
Then with barely a word,
she motions with the hockey stick

for us   to move
the pots   and bowls,
and we do,   carefully,
trying not   to spill,
making   a small path
between   them all.

See, she says. *Look at this.*
How hard must it have been for them?
Sometimes a miracle is practical.
She pats Nathan and Yael on the head,
hands Andrew the hockey stick,
then steps through the parted pots and bowls.

STARVING

After the story is over
and the songs are sung (mostly by the kids),
Uncle Paul looks up.

    I'm starving, he says. *Can't we just line up at the sink?*
And the kids nod,
already distracted.
Cousin Nathan frowning,
Yael, holding her stomach,

but Grandpa Zev puts a mighty finger
to his mouth, and his other hand on my arm.

    It's time for Rachtzah.   Memory. Connection.
    Silence, one by one.

    I rush to the kitchen
    and roll in the shining cart,
    the water in the jug
    sloshing back and forth,

the ball bearings rattling,
the levers bumping up and down.

My father glances at me,
his fingers to his lips, *Shhhhhhh.*
Grandpa Zev looks at me,
his eyes heavy as bricks.

Already, I can hear
Uncle Paul snoring
at the end of the table.
I look at my mother.
She nods to go on.

WHAT'S SUPPOSED TO HAPPEN

One box of matzah
holds the lever,
then a simple

                                      t

                          f

                i

       L

releases the string
tied to a ball bearing

the size of a giant
twirly marble that   taps
another ball bearing   that

      fa
      ll
      s
      th
      ro
      ugh
      a tu
      be

            then

                  rolls

                       down

                           a ramp

                                with enough
                                speed

            to strike the wooden lever
            that lifts and lands
            on the spigot of the water jug
                      squirting
                          out

the
perf
ect
amo
unt.

WHAT ACTUALLY HAPPENS
I lift the box of matzah,

the lever
falls
and
the
s
t
r
i
n
g
f
l
i
e
s
taps   the ball down   t h e

                                    t
                                    u
                                    b
                                    e
                                to the ramp
strikes the wooden lever
                            just right
        the water squirts
                        three times.
It works, and works, and works again
            onto my mother's hands
                        and into the bowl beneath.
Quietly she smiles
                    as the water gently falls,

but by now,
Yael and Nathan
wave their hands in the air
making beeps and bloops,
trying their hardest not to talk.
They stumble toward the machine,
pulling each other back then
                        each one reaching
        reaching   reaching   rea-pushing
pushing   pushing

               falling   falling
     right   into   the   water   jug

b-r-e-a-k-i-n-g
Major malfunction.

Their bodies smash the spigot.
          BREAK the plastic clean off,
                    the lever flying
                              into the charoset.
                         The water,
                                   free at last,
                                        starts its flood.

THE FLOOD
When we were little,
Grandpa Zev and Grandma Mae
read us a pop-up book about Noah
where the lions' mouths roared
when the page turned,
the giraffe necks folded down
so they could get inside the ark.
Two of each animal
popping up and out
as the rain pours down
filling the land.

I liked the blue pages, water
as far as the eye could see.
Grandpa Zev told us
that floods are dangerous
but maybe the Earth
needed to be washed clean.

I hope he remembers saying that to us,
because a flood is what actually happens.

WATER AS FAR AS THE EYE CAN SEE

The water gushes forth
like a firehose
emptying onto the table,
over the tablecloth
between the canyons
of the Seder Plate
     curving and pooling
        around glasses and bowls.

Stacy tries
to block the water
with her napkin,
        but it only
        makes the water angry.

Yael screams, like the table
is covered in slime.

Aunt Edie hopelessly
stacks the haggadahs.

My mom lifts the bowls,
trying to save what she can.

My father blocks
the water with napkins.

Andrew slips,
        reaches for the table,
                pulls the tablecloth
                        just right
                                so everything
                                launches into space

                        a charoset
                                bowl

```
       F
       l
   l       i

       a       p

           n       s
           d

                   s
```

        face down

        in my father's lap

Pitchers of grape juice tip over   filled with

paper frogs

sending rivers of grape blood   plague on top

of plague

        He tries to push the pots and pans

        of the Red Sea closer to the table

          to catch the water.

Little Nathan splashes

    the soaked tablecloth

      with open palms

        water spraying

          on our faces

everyone coming alive

    like mechanical arms

of a rusted robot
                    freshly oiled.
And the water keeps on
to where Uncle Paul
snorts awake,
the liquid flowing fast
from the table
down his pants
soaking the phone
until its light goes dim.
He jumps up
trying to avoid
the cascading water
launching his chair
into some of the
silvery bowls
of the Red Sea.
More water sloshes out.
        He slips,
                kicks a different pot,
                        splashes more water
                                onto the tile,
                                        the whole floor
                                                a tiny Red Sea.

AND ME?

I watch in horror,
everything gone wrong,
my heart beating
so loud it feels
like the springs might break off.
Everyone grunting and groaning,
trying not to use words
as the water washes over us.   Washes over us.

That's when I see it.
        Grandpa Zev,
                his eyes are sudden candlelight fixed on me.
                        He holds up
                              a piece of matzah
                                  he saved from
                                  the flood

and I remember . . .

        In order to break the silence
                I just need to wash my hands,
                        and then he can say the Hamotzi,
                                the prayer over the matzah,
                                        and the meal can start.

But how can we eat?
The table drowned
everyone soaked
everything washed clean away.

Washed   clean?

All of us   soaked?

All   of   us.

A DIFFERENT SCENE

Sometimes
when machines
break down
or stop working,
the only answer
is to shut the whole thing down
            and restart.

Yael and Nathan sit in Aunt Edie's lap.
Andrew dries his hair that somehow got wet.
My mom walks on a land bridge
of towels my father has thrown down.
The pots and pans turned over,
the Red Sea, run out.

Uncle Paul shows Stacy
his waterlogged phone
dripping in his hands,
and that's when it starts.

She smiles a little,
        the kind of smile
                that has a voice
                        but she won't let it out
because it's Rachtzah.
        She covers her mouth,
                holding back the sound,
                        but it's too late,

the little sound
                scampers out
                        to the other cousins,
                                who hold back the noise
                                        with both hands.

Even my mom and dad
        pretend to stay serious,
                but when my father steps over a towel,
                        sloshes into a shallow pot,

and makes the loudest
sQuisH

Grandma Mae begins to giggle. Then everyone laughs

like one big laugh
all together
being held back
with the strength
of the ancestors.

Grandpa Zev stares at me,

mmmmm   mmmmm

he says with urgency   holding up
matzah.

A GIANT'S HOWL

Well, I say, since I'm the only one who can talk,

this did NOT go how I thought it would.

Maybe it was the way I said it
or that it was a secret password
they'd been waiting for,

but there,
at the Seder table,

a sea of drenched
tablecloths
and waterlogged
elements,
the floor dotted
with towel islands,

they all let their laughter out
     like waves of pure water
         over a dry seabed,
            and the biggest laughter of all,
              like a giant's howl,
                is Grandpa Zev,
                  his body like
                    a lighthouse
                      shining
                      on us all.

RACHTZAH

Yael climbs up into
Grandpa Zev's lap,
then Nathan and Andrew
next to Grandma Mae,
until all of them are
inside the stretch
of his embrace.

I hold up a cup,
the simplest machine of all,
and pour a drop of water,
three times,
over my hands.
I feel the water
wash over me,
and it seems like
it's not just me
but all of us,
soaked and still fizzling
        but no longer broken.

Grandpa Zev
        with light in his eyes
                holds up the matzah,
                        prays,
                                and snaps off a piece to each cousin
                                                        and
                                                        finally
                                                        to me.

I hold it up, and say, simply,
Let's go eat.

MOTZEI-MATZAH

Time to eat the matzah, unleavened flatbread that our ancestors brought with them when they left Egypt. Two main reasons are provided for why matzah is eaten on Passover: (1) Because the Jewish slaves could not afford anything else, and (2) because they were so rushed when they left Egypt, they didn't have time to let the dough rise. Either way, matzah is a reminder that we were once not treated well and that we must treat *others* well now. When matzah is mentioned at the beginning of the Magid step, the Haggadah adds: "Anyone who is hungry should come and eat, anyone who is in need should join us." Once upon a time, all we had was matzah. Now we try to share it.

- *The opposite of matzah—in a way—is "chametz," which is bread that has been given enough time to rise. On Passover, tradition asks that matzah be eaten and chametz be discarded. Why do you think that is?*

- *There are many kinds of matzah: Machine-made square matzah. Handmade circular "shmurah" matzah. Soft matzah, eaten by some Jewish communities, instead of the harder stuff. Gluten-free matzah, maybe made of oat flour instead of wheat. Chocolate-covered matzah. Matzah pizza. Something so simple can be made in so many ways. Can you think of something else—one other simple thing—that can be many things?*

- *The Haggadah relays that one ancient rabbi insisted that on Passover, not only must matzah be eaten but the word "matzah" must also be spoken. Actions have power, and so do words. Are there any words in your life that you think should be spoken? Anyone you should speak them to?*

- *Think of a time you might have to leave your home in a hurry. What would you take with you and why?*

THE SMUGGLER

BY ADAM GIDWITZ

Long ago—a hundred and forty years or so—in a faraway kingdom called Russia, in a province called Lithuania, in a town so small it has disappeared from every map, there lived a woman and her four sons.

They ran an inn for the travelers who stopped in this small town, on their way between two slightly larger towns that have also disappeared from every map. The trains would stop in the small town to refuel, and people would get off to have lunch at the inn. Almost never did anyone stay the night—why would they? There was nothing to stay for.

Life was hard for this woman and her sons, but it was about to get much harder. The oldest boy, Jake, was nearly twenty-one, the age when he would be forced to join the army of the emperor, the tsar. And everyone knew that Jewish boys like Jake were taken right to the front of the lines, given a rifle, and killed almost immediately.

So their little town was disappearing, and fewer people were coming to the inn to eat, and very soon Jake would be forced to go to war.

Something needed to change.

Then, one day, a customer came through, and everything did.

The customer's name was Mr. Abelmann, and Mr. Abelmann had with him a number of copies of a book called *A Guide for Going to America*. He left a copy at the inn. "I'll be back in a few days," he said. "Read it if you get the chance." And he looked right at Jake.

Jake read the whole book in one night.

The next night, Jake gave it to the second son, but he had no interest.

So the third son, an eleven-year-old called Adam, took the book and read the whole thing in one night, too.

The fourth son was too young to read.

The book explained everything: Peddlers were needed in America to travel door-to-door, selling goods. If you did well enough, you could open a store in some small town somewhere, and bring your family over to live above it and help you run it. With the extra help, maybe you could make enough money to set up a brother with a second store, and then a third.

That sounded a lot better than living in a town that was about to disappear.

After he'd stayed up all night reading the book, Adam came into Jake's room. The sun was almost up. Jake woke with a start and said, "What's wrong?"

Adam was crying.

"What, Adam?" Jake demanded. "What happened?"

"You're going to America," said Adam.

Jake blinked many times, like he was still trying to wake up. "What?"

"I read Mr. Abelmann's book. You're going to America. You have to."

Jake said, "If I can find a way, then yes, Adam. I will. But why are you crying?"

"I can't live here without you," said Adam. And he started to cry harder.

Jake guided his little brother onto his straw mattress and put an arm around his shoulders as the boy sobbed.

⁂

A few days later, Mr. Abelmann came back.

He frowned across a table at Mama. His long Prussian mustache made a second frown over his mouth, so he looked twice as unhappy. "I had assumed your oldest boy would go. One young man."

"Yes . . ." Mama began, hesitantly.

"*Not* a young man," Mr. Abelmann nodded at Jake, "and a *boy*." He nodded in Adam's direction. "This makes things *infinitely* more difficult."

Jake cut in: "It doesn't. Adam is strong, capable, quiet, and dependable as a mule."

Adam looked at his big brother. None of this was true.

Adam was soft, and a complainer, and clumsy, and he talked too much.

"I'm sure," said Mr. Abelmann. "But getting a passport out of Russia for you would have been impossible. Getting *two* . . . a joke."

Mama's brow furrowed like the potato fields beyond town. "If getting a passport for Jake was impossible, how did you intend . . . ?"

"Smuggle him across the border," answered Mr. Abelmann. "It's just about the only way these days. We do it all the time. But for one young man! Not a young man and a child!"

"I don't like this," Mama murmured to Jake and Adam.

It wasn't going to happen. Adam was sure of it. Jake was going to leave him.

"I'm not leaving him," Jake said.

Mr. Abelmann was about to say, *Why?*

Adam wanted to say, *Why?*

But there was something so final and decisive in Jake's tone that Mr. Abelmann raised his hands in forfeit. "So we'll be smuggling you *both* across the border . . . The next question is *how.*"

Mr. Abelmann put his hands on the table, and Mama and Jake and Adam all leaned in.

"There are two methods that usually work," Mr. Abelmann said. "One is free but frightening and dangerous. The other is expensive and frightening and slightly less dangerous."

"Expensive," said Mama.

"Free," said Jake at the same time but louder.

"Jacob!" said Mama.

"Mama, I will not let you and my two other brothers starve so Adam and I can take the cushy way."

"Nothing about this is *cushy*," Mr. Abelmann murmured.

Jake turned to him and said again: "Free."

Mr. Abelmann nodded, pulled at his long mustache—and began to describe how Jake and Adam would sneak across the Prussian border in the dead of night . . .

꧁ ꧂

Late that afternoon, Jake and Adam set out. They each carried a linen pillowcase, with a stick of salt beef, an extra shirt, an extra pair of pants, and two extra pairs of socks and underwear. Jake also had a small wallet with the money that would buy them their train tickets to the port and the boat tickets to America, plus another fifty rubles for food.

Also, Adam had four pieces of matzoh, wrapped in linen.

His mother had baked it quickly, after their conversation with Mr. Abelmann. There hadn't been time for it to rise. "Just like when the Hebrews left Egypt," his mother had said as she gave him the matzoh, and then she hugged him so he wouldn't see the tears on her face. Then their brothers hugged them, crying, too.

Jake and Adam hadn't cried. They'd been too nervous. And too excited.

America. Jake and Adam said the word like some people said "Heaven." Like they'd been *told* it was real, but they'd have to see it for themselves to be sure.

❧

Jake and Adam were walking over wet ground that was in the process of freezing again in the approaching darkness of the spring night. There were woods out ahead of them. Mr. Abelmann had told them to walk due west, through the trees. They would come to fields, and then more forest. Turn right, there, to the north, and walk an hour, and then turn and walk through another forest. "If you've gone the right way, you should see red blazes on the trees. Follow those until the sun rises. By then, you'll be in Prussia."

The woods were hilly. They walked up a small rise to find large gray stones arranged like the walls of a city and a tiny kingdom of moss growing inside them. Adam stopped to marvel at it, and Jake let him. They walked back down the hill, to a wet basin, where hundreds of bright red berries hung like purses from the skinny old arms of vines.

"Will we see the red blazes soon?" Adam asked, looking at the trees for slashes of bright paint.

"In the next woods," Jake replied. "After the fields."

They reached the fields at sunset. The sky was still blue, but a bank of clouds cut across it in a perfectly straight line, and they were pink as a rose.

As they trudged over the fields, Adam's toes felt frozen in his boots. "Do you think it's true the streets are paved with gold? In America?"

Jake's long mouth went up on one side. He wiped his nose. "No, I don't think so."

"Just a few? At least *one*? Otherwise, where would the saying come from?"

"It's advertising. Advertising is big in America. They're in love with it."

The rose cloud bank had turned bright orange by the time they reached the woods on the other side of the field.

"Start looking for the red blazes," Jake instructed Adam.

"Like the blood over the doors when the Hebrews fled Egypt," said Adam. "Trying to get to the promised land."

Jake grinned. "My little brother the poet."

Adam beamed. "Like Moses and Aaron when they—"

"OK, don't overdo it."

Adam closed his mouth.

He thought of the matzoh Mama had made for them, but he didn't think it was the right time to ask Jake if they could stop and eat.

Suddenly, Jake hissed, "Shhh!"

In the distance ahead of them were two torches. Suddenly, a dog barked. They heard a voice shout in Russian: "Ivan, this way! The dog smells someone!"

Jake turned to Adam and whispered, "Run!"

He and Adam ran west, toward the border with Prussia. The dog got closer. The shouts got louder. And the night got darker.

They came to another hill. "It's too slow to run up it," Jake hissed, and he pulled Adam left, to go around. Running in the woods in the dark is nearly impossible—fallen logs, breaking sticks, vines that wrap around your ankles, thorns in your face. They moved as fast as they could, Jake and Adam, but the dog was gaining on them, and the men with the torches were shouting, "Smugglers! You're under arrest! In the name of the tsar!"

Jake grabbed Adam and pulled him hard, down, into a large divot—almost a cave—under a large rock. "Hide!" Jake whispered.

"No!" Adam hissed back. Suddenly, he was opening the pillowcase he'd been carrying.

"What are you doing?!"

Adam didn't answer. He rummaged past the extra shirt and two pairs of underwear. The matzoh was broken into pieces inside the linen. But next to that was the stick of salt beef. He dropped it on the ground. "For the dog," he said. "Now go!" And they started to run again.

A moment later, the dog's frantic barking had stopped. Jake and Adam looked over their shoulders to see the two torches, also stopped. The men were shouting: "What has he got? Is it the smuggler? A shoe?"

"No, salt beef!"

"What? Where did he get that? Stupid dog!"

"Don't talk about my dog that way!"

"Maybe feed him before we go on patrol then!"

As the two voices argued in Russian, Jake and Adam ran.

It was very late at night now. The brothers had walked for hours since losing the border patrolmen and the dog—but they had no idea where they were.

"I . . . I'm sorry," Adam moaned.

"You're sorry for what?" Jake demanded. "You got us away from the dog . . ."

Adam fell.

Jake rushed to his side. "What's wrong?!"

"I'm sorry. I'm trying. But I can't keep walking." And then: "I'm letting you down. I don't want to let you down."

Jake shushed Adam. "Let's sleep here. We're lost anyway. I haven't seen a single red blaze the whole time. We'll figure out where we are in the morning."

"I'm sorry . . ."

Jake curled his body, strong and warm, around his little brother and held him in the cold. "There's nothing to be sorry for. And Adam?"

"Yes?"

"You couldn't let me down if you tried."

"Jake?"

"Yes?"

"We're like the Hebrews, lost in the desert."

"Enough with the poetry."

They fell asleep, half covered with leaves, smiling.

☙

They woke when the sun rose—and saw, through the morning mist, their village.

"We're not in Prussia," said Adam.

Jake put his head in his hands. "No. We're back home."

☙

"So, the expensive way," said Mr. Abelmann.

They were sitting at a table in the inn again. Mr. Abelmann had stayed the night, to be sure everything went well. Which, clearly, it had not.

"I suppose," Jake replied, a very sour look on his face. He glanced at Mama. She made a gesture with her hand and her lips that said, *It's OK. We'll be OK.* Jake pressed his lips together and shook his head. But he listened as Mr. Abelmann explained the expensive way:

"Now that the new tsar has made books practically illegal here in Lithuania, there has arisen a network of book smugglers, operating between Königsberg, in Prussia, and Vilnius, the Lithuanian capital. They're not Jewish, these smugglers, but I trust them. I trust anyone who sells books for a living. You know they have no ambition to be rich." Mr. Abelmann smiled, and his mustache went down while the corners of his mouth went up. "Since they don't make much money from books, they supplement their income by taking people across the border."

"How much?" Jake demanded.

"One hundred rubles. Per person."

Jake threw his head back and laughed. He said to Mama, "You'll starve!"

"We'll be fine," said Mama. "I will not send you to the tsar's army for you to get shot invading the Ottoman Empire or wherever. I'd rather starve."

Jake rubbed his eyes as he said to Mr. Abelmann: "A hundred rubles per person. Do these book smugglers negotiate?"

Mr. Abelmann said, "A hundred rubles per person is *after* we negotiate."

⁂

Mr. Abelmann left, and he came back a week later with a man who looked like a poet. Adam had never met a real poet, but the moment he saw this man, he knew he'd met one at last. The poet had a beard with a mustache waxed into points. Under his long leather traveling jacket he wore a velvet suit jacket and green tweed pants. He looked ridiculous.

But he'd brought a horse and a cart, and despite being a poet, he was all business.

145

"Usually," he said as he walked around his cart with Jake and Adam, Mama following anxiously behind, "I'd have you get in burlap sacks, surround you with hay, and say you were potatoes. But we've used that a lot recently, and since you run an inn . . . I assume you make your own beer?"

"Yes . . ." said Jake guardedly.

"So, do you have any spare vats?"

"We don't have *anything* to spare," Jake replied curtly. "You're already taking two hundred rubles. You need *more*?"

The poet looked hurt. "I'm trying to *help* you. Yes, we charge, but you wouldn't ask me to risk five years in the tsar's army for free, would you?"

"We have an old vat," Adam piped up. "It's rusted through . . ."

"Rusted through won't work," the poet said.

" . . . but just on the bottom."

"Oho! I stand corrected!" the poet exclaimed.

Jake frowned at Adam. But Mama was already leading the poet toward the old vat.

An hour later, the rusted beer vat was in the back of the cart. And Adam and Jake were inside it.

"Good thing you're both small," the poet said, looking down at them.

"Big enough to stand up and knock your block off," Jake grumbled.

The poet frowned at Jake. "I get that you don't like this, and you don't particularly like me—though I'm not sure why."

"I have about two hundred reasons . . ."

The poet shrugged. "OK, I understand. But listen. If the border guards find you, don't threaten to knock their blocks off. They'll take the opportunity to shoot a Jew, if you offer it."

Mama, standing beside the poet, let out a gasp and smacked him hard across his shoulder.

"I'm sorry, Ma'am. Truth is beauty, beauty truth. And while the truth may not set you free, it might just keep your sons alive."

Jake and Adam stood for a last round of embraces with their family. Mama held Jake for a long time, and whispered, "Please, take care of Adam. But don't forget to take care of yourself, too." And then, when she hugged Adam, she said into his ear, "Help him to keep smiling." Adam swallowed a lump in his throat the size of a potato and promised he would.

Then they got back into the vat and the lid was closed and knocked tight with a mallet.

"Can you breathe in there?" the poet asked.

"Yes," Jake said.

"It smells like mold and beer," Adam added.

Mama wept and put her head beside the barrel and whispered, *"We love you."*

And they were off.

It was a bumpy, uncomfortable ride. The roads were all mud and rock, and the cart shook side to side violently. Jake and Adam both smacked their heads against the side of the vat over and over, until they had ringing headaches and felt like the bells in a church tower.

After two hours, the cart slowed, then stopped. Then it started again. Then stopped. Then started.

Adam wanted to ask Jake what he thought was happening, but he didn't dare make a sound.

Finally, they heard voices.

"Where're you going?" In Russian.

"Königsberg."

"Why?"

"I live there."

When they heard the Russian voice again, it was much closer. "What's back here?"

"Beer," said the poet.

"Beer? You're bringing Lithuanian beer into Prussia?" The border guard sounded skeptical. Adam stopped breathing. Jake slowly reached out and took his hand. "You think the Germans will *drink* this stuff?"

The poet replied, quick as the flick of a pen, "I think the Germans will drink anything."

The border guard laughed. Adam relaxed. Jake let go of his hand.

And then they heard someone climbing up into the cart. "You wouldn't happen to be hiding anything in this beer vat, would you?"

Adam and Jake both stopped breathing again.

The poet said: "Like what?"

"Books," said the border guard.

Silence.

Then the poet laughed. "Who brings books *to* Prussia? Don't the smugglers take them the other way?"

"Ah, you're right," said the guard. He moved away from the vat.

Adam started to breathe again.

"Got a crowbar?"

"Good God," Jake exhaled.

"Figure I should just open the vat and check. Just to be safe. Don't want to get in trouble with my boss. He's a real swine."

"Nope!" said the poet too cheerfully. "No crowbar. I pick it up sealed and deliver it sealed. They wouldn't trust me with a vat full of beer otherwise." He forced a laugh.

"So you don't actually *know* it's beer in here," said the Russian guard. "Could be anything. Could be gunpowder. Could be explosives."

Silence.

"Hey, Petrovich!" the guard called suddenly. "Bring the crowbar!" Then, to the poet, he said, "For your safety, as much as mine."

Adam and Jake locked eyes in the near total dark. Jake reached into his pocket. Adam had begun to shiver. He tried not to make the vat shake.

"Here," said a new voice. The guard moved closer to the vat. They heard him jam the crowbar under the lid. Metal groaned. Jake took his hand from his pocket.

POP!

Adam shielded his eyes. Gray light streamed into the vat. Jake raised his arm.

Adam, blinded by the sudden daylight, couldn't see what was happening.

He heard the lid of the vat sliding . . . back into place.

They were in the dark again.

The border guard jumped down from the cart. He said to the poet, "You can keep 'em. We don't want their kind here."

The cart rolled forward.

Adam whispered, "What happened?"

Jake whispered back, "Now we have fifty rubles less, and they have two less Jews in Russia." Jake shook his head in the dark. "I have no idea how we'll eat now."

Adam reached into his pillowcase. There was the linen. Wrapped around eight new pieces of matzoh. Unbroken. He took two out and handed one to Jake.

They ate the matzoh as the poet steered them into another country, on the way to a new promised land.

MAROR

Step eight: eating maror, the bitter herb. Maror is one of several things placed on the Seder Plate throughout the night, alongside Karpas, charoset, and other foods. Eating maror—to remember the bitterness of slavery—is among the most ancient of Passover traditions, mentioned in the Torah (the Jewish Bible) right alongside eating matzah.

- *For this step, maror is dipped in a little charoset. Bitter into sweet. Why do you think that is?*

- *There is no universal vegetable used for maror. Many Jews use horseradish, which was popular in Europe. And many use something else—romaine lettuce, endive—because horseradish may not have been used in ancient times. What food would you choose as the bitter herb?*

- *Much of the food and drink at the Seder is consumed while leaning to the side (a symbol of freedom, relief, or relaxation), but not maror. Why might that be?*

- *The Passover story begins with bitterness (symbolized by maror) and ends with freedom (symbolized by the matzah). You'd think, then, that maror would be eaten before the matzah. And there are different explanations for why it's the other way around. Maybe it's just because that's the order the foods are mentioned in the Torah. Maybe it's because freedom is never perfect; sometimes there's a little bitterness mixed in. And maybe it's a warning: Don't waste your freedom. Don't take advantage of it. Because it's not guaranteed, and bitterness can always return. Why do you think maror is eaten at this stage of the Seder, after the matzah?*

THE BITTER PRINCESS

BY SOFIYA PASTERNACK

"Once upon a time," Daniel said, walking down the front steps of his tenement building, "in a faraway land, there was—"

"A princess!" Daniel's little sister, Rahela, said. She clapped her hands, and even though Daniel was annoyed by her interrupting, and a little annoyed at having to take her with him to the market so Mama could finish cleaning, he smiled at her excitement as she followed him down the street. A streetcar rumbled by, gears cranking and exhaust billowing into the air. Daniel waved his hand to try to disperse the exhaust, and when that did nothing, he pulled off his cap and used that instead. The cap worked better than his hand had, and as soon as the air was cleared—well, as cleared as it could be on a stuffy Monday afternoon surrounded by frantic adults getting their last preparations for Pesach done—he stuck the cap back over his brown hair.

"Yes," he said. "A princess. Do you remember how to say it?"

"No," Rahela stated without even trying.

"*Prinţesă.*" Daniel's annoyance returned, this time about Rahela not knowing Mama and Tata's language. But he smoothed it away like he had his feelings about her interrupting. She always interrupted the story of the Bitter Princess so she could half-tell it herself, and she'd barely spoken Romanian at all when they moved to New York City. She probably didn't remember their *bunică* sitting them down to tell them the story of the Bitter Princess. She claimed to not remember their home at all. When Daniel closed his eyes and tried to pull up images of what their house had looked like, or even what the city of Iași looked like, everything was fuzzy and fading, replaced with the chaos of their tenement building on Orchard Street and Delancey. He was twelve and had lived in New York City for only four years, but even so he was forgetting his home. Soon, he'd be like Rahela and have no memory of it at all.

Rahela said, "That's what I said. *Prințesă*," and grinned. On her eighth birthday, she had lost a tooth, and the new tooth hadn't grown in enough to fill the gap in her smile.

"*Bravo*," Daniel said, and continued, "The princess spent her days inside her castle, walking the halls and trying to remember something she had forgotten. But the prince always said, 'No, no, you didn't forget anything. You're perfectly happy. Stop worrying.'"

"He's a *liar*!" Rahela yelled.

"Liar!" Daniel yelled with her. The siblings navigated the crowded sidewalk, dodging around pushcarts and pedestrians and several boys Daniel knew from shul, each carrying a huge box of matzah from Streit's. One of the big Streit's trucks was parked up the street off to the side, with a long line forming. They gave away free matzah every Pesach for people who couldn't afford to buy it, and every Pesach that Daniel had spent in New York, his family had needed the free matzah from Streit's. Daniel scoured his memory of the tenement's little kitchen, trying to remember if he'd seen any of their own matzah boxes this year and hoping that maybe they didn't need free matzah anymore.

Rahela looked up at him with big, waiting eyes. "The princess met a witch," she prompted.

"Yes, she did," Daniel said. "One day an old woman stood outside the princess's window and told the princess she was very hungry. The princess went to the kitchen and took the only thing that was there: a sweet biscuit. When she handed the biscuit to the old woman, the old woman handed her back three pieces of root."

Rahela scoffed. "I wouldn't trade a cookie for a disgusting bunch of bitter roots!"

"Well, she didn't know they were bitter yet, did she? Plus, they were *magic* roots."

Rahela sniffed. "If she didn't know they were bitter, she wouldn't have known they were magic, either."

"Oh, hush and listen." Daniel extended three of his fingers and wiggled them with fake menace. In his best old-lady voice, he said, "To recall what you've forgotten, eat one root at sunset for the next three sunsets when there are three stars in the sky." He let out a high-pitched witchy cackle. "And then, *poof!* She was gone!"

"And she took the cookie," Rahela said, shaking her head.

"She took the cookie." Daniel would have continued the story, but something nagged at him. He asked, "Rahela, do you remember *Bunică*?"

"Who?"

"Grandma," he specified in English.

"Oh." Rahela was quiet for a moment. "No."

"She used to make us cookies," Daniel said as they finally cleared the crowd around the Streit's truck.

Rahela kicked at a piece of paper that fluttered across the sidewalk. "Did the princess eat the bitter roots?"

Daniel sighed. Back to the story. "The princess wasn't sure if she should eat the roots. What if the witch was an evil witch? What if the roots were poisonous? Or cursed?" Daniel shrugged as they reached the corner of Orchard Street, and he grasped Rahela's hand in his to keep her from getting swept away in the crowd of people and pushcarts. He looked up and down the street, searching for the pushcart his mother had sent him after. He didn't see it right away, so he headed up the sidewalk, falling in with the crowd bustling through the late March afternoon.

"Daniel?" Rahela asked, barely audible over the noise of the street.

"What?"

"Did she eat the roots?"

Daniel had told Rahela this story several times—just like *Bunică* had told him this story several times—so she knew exactly what the princess did. She knew just what happened next. But there was something about the telling of the story, not just the story itself, he supposed, so he said, "She did. That night, when there were three stars in the sky, she ate the first root. And *ugh!* It was so bitter and terrible, she almost spat it out."

"She can't spit it out!" Rahela argued. "Or it won't be magic!"

Daniel nodded. "Well, she didn't spit it out. She ate it, even though it was so bitter, and you know what happened?"

Rahela shouted, "What happened?"

"She remembered something!" Daniel said. "She remembered a red dress, even though she had no red dresses of her own."

"I'd like a red dress," Rahela said.

Daniel spotted the pushcart he sought through the crowd, and he changed direction toward it as he said, "One day, I'll buy you a red dress."

"I'll look very pretty in a red dress," she said, not seeming to understand that Daniel would have to be unreasonably rich to buy her a red dress. But he agreed that she would look very pretty in a red dress as they approached the little vegetable cart and the boisterous man behind it.

"Well, well!" Daniel's father boomed. Tata was a big man with a thick accent and ruddy cheeks, and he came out from behind the cart to pick up Rahela and throw her in the air. She screamed with glee, and he set her back down on the ground gently before he razzed Daniel's cap over his hair. "Did your mama send you?" Tata asked in English. He spoke English as much as he could with Daniel and Rahela, to make them practice, even though Tata wasn't very good at it.

Daniel nodded, and Tata pulled three packages from behind the cart. The first was a small package wrapped in newspaper, which he handed to Rahela. "My little bird, I got these from Yitzhak this morning. Can you be in charge of them?"

Rahela nodded and took the package, then sniffed it. She made a face.

Tata laughed. "It's . . ." He cocked his head to the side like he always did when he couldn't remember a word. "*Amar*. Daniel."

Daniel was still staring at the other two packages: matzah boxes from Streit's. "Bitter."

Tata snapped his fingers. "Bitter." He pinched Rahela's cheek and said, "Not like you, though. Be careful you don't make it sweet."

Daniel took the matzah packages from his father, one under each arm.

Tata kissed Rahela on the top of her head and then squeezed Daniel's shoulder. "Go straight home, eh?" Tata said. "Mama probably needs help with chametz."

Rahela groaned loudly as Daniel let out a soft sigh. The tenement wasn't difficult to clean because it was big—it wasn't; it was very, very small—but because before Pesach, Mama always decided it had gotten dirty overnight, no matter how well they'd cleaned it the day before, and no matter how clean it still looked. They said goodbye to Tata so he could go back to selling from the pushcart and carefully navigated the crowded street toward home.

They walked quietly until they were away from the crowd, and then Rahela said, "She told the prince about the red dress, of course."

"Of course," Daniel said, adjusting the matzah boxes under his arms. "And the prince told her he had never seen her wear a red dress and that she must have had a dream or something."

"Liar!" Rahela said with quiet anger.

"She didn't think it was a dream," Daniel said. "She thought maybe she had to prove it to him. And the next night when there were three stars in the sky, she ate the second root, and it was even more bitter than the first. It was so bitter she almost couldn't finish it. But she remembered a second thing just then!"

"A white knife," Rahela said. "A red dress with a white knife."

Daniel was about to continue the story—to tell of the prince still not believing her and begging her not to eat the third root—when he heard a cry from somewhere nearby.

He stopped, swiveling his head around. The crowd wasn't as thick here as it was out on Orchard. The brick tenements had narrow alleys between them, where debris from the ground floor sweatshops and trash from the apartments above them was piled up sometimes, and as Daniel paused, he heard another cry coming from one of the alleys, and he ran toward it.

"Daniel?" Rahela called from the sidewalk, and he stopped at the alley mouth. Closer now, he could make out a group of boys past a haphazard stack of extra bricks and some trash. One of the boys was covering his head and cowering away from the other three, who all took turns hitting him. The one getting hit wore a kippah, and as Daniel watched, one of the other boys ripped the kippah off the boy's head and threw it to the ground.

Daniel turned, shoving the matzah boxes into Rahela's hands, and he whispered, "Run home, Rahela. As fast as you can. Do you understand?"

Rahela's eyes were wide and furious, and Daniel knew better than to give her the chance to argue. He turned away from her and ran into the alley, standing as tall as he could and shouting, "Hey!"

The bullies turned to see who was yelling, and Daniel studied their faces to see if he recognized them. Not a one. They weren't from the East Side. Heart pounding so hard he could hear the rush of blood in his ears, he said, "You don't belong here."

The largest of the bullies sneered at Daniel and pointed to the other boy, still on the ground. "Yeah? Well neither does he. He oughta go back to Poland and take his whole stupid family with him." He looked Daniel up and down as he took slow, careful steps toward him. "You Polish?"

Daniel curled his hands into fists. "What's that matter?"

"So you are?" The bully continued to approach.

"If I am, if I'm not," Daniel said, "doesn't matter. Leave him alone, or else."

The bully was right there, up close, and he said, "Or else . . . what?"

Before Daniel could think of what else, something flew through the air and hit the bully square in the face.

"Ow!" the bully yelled.

As the object bounced off the bully, Daniel smelled the unmistakable bitter scent of the maror.

The bully looked where the maror had come from, face pulled into a snarl. "Hey, what's the—*ow!*"

Another root hit him in the eye this time. Daniel turned to see Rahela standing where he'd left her, matzah boxes at her feet, maror package ripped open. She had the last root in her fist, and her arm cranked back, ready to throw it.

"*My eye!*" the bully yelled, clutching at his face. "She hit me in the eye!"

"Go cry to your mama!" Rahela thundered.

It wasn't until one of the bullies said, "What the heck does *that* mean?" that Daniel realized Rahela had yelled in Romanian.

The two remaining bullies looked at each other, like they were trying to decide what to do with this absurd little girl hefting smelly roots, and one took a step toward her. As he did, Rahela looked behind her and yelled in English, "We're in here, officer! Right here!" and waved her arm in the air.

"She called the cops!" one of the bullies yelped, and the three of them fled the other way down the alley.

Rahela hesitated, root clutched in her fist, and then she chucked it after the fleeing bullies. It bounced on the ground in the dirty alley, vanishing into the layer of trash there. She picked up the matzah boxes as she stomped toward Daniel. He searched the alley behind her for the police, but there was no one there.

"You didn't call anyone," Daniel said, not believing Rahela had defeated three bullies with some maror and a lie about police.

She shoved the matzah boxes at him. "So?"

Daniel grabbed the boxes and clutched them to his chest. "I told you to run home."

"Good thing I don't listen to you, isn't it?" Rahela said as she went over to where the other boy was still kneeling on the ground and tenderly touching his lip, which had been split open. He looked up at her with wonderment and only blinked slowly in response when she asked, "Are you okay?"

Daniel went to follow his sister to where she stood over the boy but stopped when he saw the two pieces of maror on the ground. Both pieces had been stepped on and smashed up and had alley grime ground into them. Even so, Daniel set down the two boxes of matzah and swept the smashed maror into his palm, then tucked the herb into his trouser pocket. Then he picked up the matzah boxes and went behind Rahela as she retrieved the boy's kippah from the ground, dusted it off, and handed it to him. He hesitated, then took it from her, standing as he smoothed it over his dirty hair.

Daniel didn't know any Polish, and he expected a Polish boy wouldn't know Romanian, so he tried to communicate in the language of the East Side. In Yiddish, he asked, "What's your name?"

The boy looked surprised, and then replied in Yiddish. "My name is Michał."

"I'm Daniel," he said, extending a hand to Michał to shake. "And this is my sister, Rahela."

Michał shook Daniel's hand and regarded Rahela with awe. "You have good aim."

Rahela puffed her chest out and stuck both hands on her hips. "Thanks."

Michał tried to smile, but his split lip made him wince instead. Daniel said, "We live right down here," and pointed vaguely in the direction of his tenement. "Where do you live?"

Michał blinked wet, shining eyes and said in a deceptively steady voice, "I'm not sure. We just came here."

"From Poland?"

Michał nodded. "Poznań."

"I bet Mama knows where the new Polish are," Rahela said. "Come on, Michał." And she turned from the alley, marching back toward the sidewalk, and Daniel shrugged at Michał. They followed, and out on the sidewalk, Rahela walked ahead for only a few moments before she slowed to Daniel's side and said to Michał, "Daniel was telling me a fairy tale before we heard you in the alley. Now he has to finish it." She shrugged as if to say she was sorry, and there was nothing she could do about the situation.

Daniel looked at Rahela, and she glanced up at him before moving her gaze back to the sidewalk. Rahela, who pretended not to speak Romanian, but did. And pretended not to remember their home. But maybe . . .

"Okay," Daniel said, and had to pause to find the words he needed. He'd never told the story in Yiddish before. "Um, so the third day, the princess told the prince again about the bitter roots and the memories, and he begged her to stop. He said the root being even more bitter meant that it was poison, and if she ate the third root, she would surely die."

"*Die*," Rahela said, dramatically throwing her head back and making a choking sound.

Daniel felt silly with Michał watching the theatrics, but he continued anyway. "The princess waited until the third star was in the sky that night, and she ate half of the third root. It was more and more bitter with every bite, and she started to feel ill. The prince ran up to her and said he was right, it was poison, and she must give the root to him and stop eating it! But instead of handing it over, the princess ate the last bit of the bitterest root, even though her stomach was sick and her eyes teared."

Rahela made a retching sound, then threw her hands into the air and announced, "But she didn't die!"

"She didn't die!" Daniel announced in agreement. "The spell over her was broken, and the enchantment melted away. She had been a magical prisoner, and as she remembered the third thing—a majestic black horse—the prince transformed into the horse. He was her loyal warhorse and had been enchanted in order to keep her trapped in her castle of forgetting who she really was, so her enemies could take her kingdom. But since she remembered, she put on her red dress and picked up her white knife, which was actually a sword, and she jumped on the back of her black warhorse, and she took back her kingdom."

Rahela crowed, "Took it back!" just as they reached the door of their tenement. Inside, the hall was dim and stuffy, and the ever-present noise of the sweatshops hummed through the air. Daniel reached for the door handle, but before he could open it, the door swung in, and Mama huffed in English, "Well, it's about time—"

But she stopped when she noticed Michał and his cut lip, and her eyes got huge. "Danny, what happened? Who is this?"

In Yiddish, Daniel said, "This is Michał, Mama. He just got here from Poland, and some boys were beating him up, and he doesn't know where his family lives. Can you—"

But Mama was already sweeping the three of them into the cleaned tenement, tasking Rahela with fetching a bucket of water from the spout in the back. Mama then began heating the water over the tiny stove and cleaning Michał's lip. As she did, Daniel sat at her side, watching, and he said, "Mama, we dropped the maror."

Mama slowed in her cleaning of Michał's lip for a moment.

"But it's okay." Daniel reached into his pocket, digging out the maror for the Seder, all smashed apart and flecked with alley grime. "I can clean it up. It's crushed but it'll still work." Daniel tried to pick the grime and grit out of the ground-up bitter herb, but it was too well smashed in. He kept picking anyway. Maybe he could still save it. He knew they didn't have the money to waste on more.

Mama put her hand over Daniel's.

He looked up at her, eyes burning. "Mama, I can—"

"Oh, hush," she said tenderly, and she gently slid the ruined maror away from him.

Mama sent Rahela to ask some of the other women who lived in the tenement where the new Polish were mostly living, and by the time Tata got home, Michał's own tata had come to get him. Mama insisted that Michał and his family come for the first night.

As Daniel's mama and tata negotiated Seder plans with Michał's relieved tata, the boys stood outside in the hallway.

"That story about the princess and the bitter roots . . ." Michał said. "Is that from Romania?"

Daniel shrugged, and before he could answer, Rahela swooped from around the corner and said, "Bubbe told it to us."

Daniel put his hands on his hips. "So, you *do* remember?"

Rahela nodded. "I remember, at the end every time, she'd

say that remembering can be bitter but forgetting is a prison." She crossed her arms over her belly. "I thought if I forgot about the nice things, like our house and the forest and the flowers, then I could forget about . . . the bad things."

Daniel swallowed hard as he remembered his home: the beautiful landscapes, the spacious streets, the big houses—but also the suspicious looks, the angry shouting, the sour fear when Mama would wake him up and shush him as she took Daniel and Rahela to hide from the men outside.

Rahela said, "But that's not how remembering works."

Michał's tata emerged from the tenement, and they left.

Two days later, on the first night of Pesach, Michał and his tata came back, and they had his mama and two sisters with them. Daniel watched Michał hand Rahela a newspaper-wrapped package as his family went inside the tenement.

Rahela unwrapped the newspaper, revealing the bitter maror inside, and Michał said, "I'm glad you remembered."

"Şi mie," Rahela said in Romanian.

Me too.

KORECH

The next step is Korech: Eating a sandwich, made of matzah and maror (and maybe some charoset, too). All eaten together, to remember the practice of a famous ancient sage named Hillel, who did exactly that—and maybe to remind ourselves that little in life is all or nothing; good or bad; freedom or bitterness. We all live with a bit of both.

- *Are there any other two things you can think of that seem like they wouldn't go together—but do anyway?*

- *Hillel is most often remembered for his kindness (and for his famous sandwich). What do you want to be remembered for?*

- *What is your favorite sandwich in the whole world? (Besides matzah and maror, of course.)*

- *Have you ever felt sandwiched between two different things? Two friends? Two family members? Two lives?*

GROWING UP SANDWICHED BETWEEN IDENTITIES

BY RUTH BEHAR

Passover united and also divided our family. It was on Passover that I came to understand I wasn't simply Jewish and Cuban, or "Juban," as we are sometimes called. In addition to those two identities, I was split at the root in yet another way.

Every year, Passover reminded me I was a child of two distinct Jewish ways of looking at the world. On the first night, the Seder was hosted by Baba and Zeide, who were Ashkenazi. On the second night, the Seder was hosted by Abuela and Abuelo, who were Sephardic.

When I was growing up, I didn't use the words "Ashkenazi" and "Sephardic" to describe my grandparents. I used the words that were used in Cuba. Baba and Zeide were "polacos"— Polish. Abuela and Abuelo were "turcos"—Turkish.

But Zeide was actually Russian. People just didn't distinguish between Polish and Russian in Cuba. Baba and Zeide thought of themselves as "yiddishe." They spoke Yiddish and believed this was one of the key features of a Jewish identity.

Abuela and Abuelo were born in Turkey, but their ancestry was Spanish, going back five centuries to the expulsion from Spain in 1492, so they thought of themselves as "espanyoles." They didn't speak Yiddish, which Baba and Zeide found strange at first, not having ever met Jews who weren't from Eastern Europe. Instead, Abuela and Abuelo spoke Ladino or Judeo-Spanish, an old Spanish mixed with Italian, French, Turkish, and languages from their various diasporas that they wrote in Hebrew letters. For Sephardic Jews, to speak Spanish is to speak a Jewish language; it is one of the ways that an ancestral tie to Jewish Spain is claimed to this day.

Each set of grandparents had a different history, a different culture, a different language—they were equally Jewish and yet very differently Jewish.

What united our whole family was how fiercely everyone embraced the notion that on Passover we don't simply remember but *relive* the miracle of how our ancestors fled Egypt to escape slavery.

This reliving always happened with lots of drama and lots of feeling. It was truly as if we'd been there all those centuries ago and experienced the Exodus ourselves.

We were people who had fled our home in search of freedom.

People who believed the sea would part long enough for us to get across to the other side.

I was four and a half when my family made the decision to leave Cuba. It was a painful decision. They loved Cuba, thought it was paradise. My four Jewish grandparents had fled Europe and found a home in Cuba on the eve of the Holocaust, when millions of Jews perished. Cuba gave them the gift of life. They had children, and their children had children, and they expected to stay forever.

But then Fidel Castro came to power and quickly turned into a dictator after promising to bring democracy to all Cubans. My family, like many others, didn't want to remain in a country that stole away their freedom.

As a child, I became part of the exodus of fifteen thousand Jews who left Cuba to begin anew in the United States. I was too young to understand why we had to leave, let alone in such a hurry. All I knew was that Castro was like the mean king Pharaoh who had made life miserable for the Jewish people.

I didn't realize we were leaving forever. My mother did. She was in tears as she packed the family photographs. Those fleeing Cuba could take only one suitcase. Somehow she thought to bring my blue school uniform, which had a Jewish star embroidered on the pocket over my heart. I attended— for a few brief months—the Jewish day school in Havana that she had attended. Classes were taught in Spanish and Yiddish. I still speak Spanish today, but I lost the Yiddish after we left Cuba.

My childhood in Cuba ended so abruptly, I didn't have a chance to say goodbye to the girl who'd once lived on a tropical island. One day I woke up in Israel, on a kibbutz, where we lived for a year after fleeing Cuba, and a year later

I woke up in New York, struggling to learn English, make new friends, and get used to snowy winters. Being an immigrant kid wasn't easy. But as my family often reminded me, my life would have been worse if we'd stayed in Cuba. I had clothes, I had food, I had a roof over my head. Most of all, I had freedom. Once I got good at English, and after suffering a year in a body cast as a result of a terrible car accident, I became a bookworm. I had the freedom to read any book I wanted from the Bookmobile that appeared like magic in our working-class neighborhood of identical sad brick buildings. In Cuba, I was reminded, I would have been told what I could and couldn't read.

Each year, when our family sat down to celebrate Passover, there was a lot of talk about freedom and how lucky we were to be in a free country. We had sacrificed, left a home we loved, to find freedom. When we read from the Haggadah about our ancestors having so little time for the bread to rise that they brought matzah with them on their journey, we understood. And we understood about bitter tears. In our dreams, we cried for the lost country where the air tasted of salt.

❧

I adored all four of my grandparents and was blessed to know them. But I was closer to Baba and Zeide, who were Mami's parents. They spoke Yiddish to each other and called me "shayne meidele" (sweet girl), which warmed my heart. I saw them often because we all lived in the same brick building in Queens and my mother was very close to them.

Abuela and Abuelo, after leaving Cuba via Jamaica, went to live in Canarsie, in Brooklyn, where many Sephardic Jews from Cuba settled. Papi didn't like Canarsie. He never said why, preferring to be among Ashkenazi Jews who didn't understand how he could be Jewish and not have grown up speaking Yiddish. Perhaps he kept his distance because he didn't get along with his father, toward whom he held a grudge because Abuelo had forced him to go peddling in Havana to help support the family, not allowing him to fulfill his dream of studying architecture. Whatever the reason, we didn't see Abuelo or Abuela very often, so their traditions seemed mysterious to me. I remember how Abuela scolded Papi for not visiting enough; he'd lower his head and get embarrassed like a little boy.

Passover would arrive, and because we celebrated the first Seder at Baba and Zeide's house, I came to feel, as a child, that the Ashkenazi traditions must be more important than the Sephardic traditions. They came first, after all. These distinctions made by my family mirrored the way Ashkenazi traditions of being Jewish were dominant in American culture. Bagels were everywhere, not the sesame-topped Sephardic biscuits known as bizcochos. Jewishness was represented in artistic works such as *Fiddler on the Roof*, not in the melancholy Sephardic love songs preserved through multiple diasporas that Abuela had once sung, strumming on a Turkish oud left behind in Cuba. I struggled to embrace both the Ashkenazi and Sephardic Seders and not treat one as superior to the other. Because I loved both sets of grandparents, I looked beyond the messages of inequality, though I couldn't help seeing the Ashkenazi Seder as the "normal Seder" and the Sephardic Seder as the "exotic Seder."

At that Ashkenazi Seder, we'd form a bridge of folding tables to create one long snake to fit my parents, my brother and I, my mother's older sister and my uncle and cousins, my mother's younger brother and my aunt, and Baba's younger sister and my great-uncle. Often more aunts, uncles, and cousins would attend, if in town, and we'd squeeze together happily.

We ate gefilte fish that Baba made from scratch. It was the best gefilte fish ever. Even my father, who hates gefilte fish (it's not a traditional food among Sephardic Jews), would eat it. There was a fish shop where Baba bought fresh carp, whitefish, and pike and she'd have them chop it with onions. Then she'd take the chopped fish to her kitchen and shape it into a loaf that she baked, cooled, sliced, and served on little dishes. Her gefilte fish was especially good topped with the pungent horseradish that also served as our bitter herb in the Seder (how truly bitter it tasted on its own!). She made the fluffiest matzoh balls, soft as marshmallows. Then there was roasted chicken, potato kugel, and tzimmes made of sweet carrots and plump raisins. The dessert was baked apples, which we kids found too mushy. Zeide always went to the Jewish bakery and got a chocolate rainbow cake for us, with a pink top layer and a green bottom layer. We loved it because it was so colorful.

I don't know how Baba found time to do all that cooking. She was in her sixties and worked six days a week, along with Zeide, at a fabric store on Roosevelt Avenue, underneath the rattle of the train, which gave her headaches, and she took English classes at night and read the Yiddish newspaper cover to cover before going to bed. She preferred to be smart and sharp, rather than pretty and nice, and I thought that was great. Still, she insisted on preparing our Passover meal.

Zeide led the Seder in Hebrew. He was shy and had a soft, whispery voice. You had to lift your ears to hear him. My brother, Mori, my cousins Danny and Linda, and I each read aloud one of the Four Questions. When we came to the end of the Seder, everyone got a spoonful of the haroset, made out of chunks of apple mixed with walnuts, a bit of horseradish, and a piece of matzoh. That was the korech sandwich. Our Seder would end without too much fanfare.

We kids would scarf down the meal Baba had taken so much time to prepare. We were eager to be done to go in search of the afikomen. Zeide hid the afikomen really well. To find it, we had to peer into every nook and cranny of their one-bedroom apartment. We competed feverishly and sometimes none of us found it, though Zeide made sure to give each of us a prize—a crisp one-dollar bill, a lot of money at that time. And then we'd stay up late, the grown-ups tipsy on Manischewitz wine, telling jokes and remembering Cuba while nibbling on coconut macaroons that came in cans. "Remember how good the dulce de coco tasted in Cuba?" someone would say. "We'll never eat coconut sweets like that again," someone would reply. And then we'd say buenas noches.

The next night, the second night of Passover, which Jews in Israel don't celebrate, we'd go to Canarsie, just the four of us—Papi, Mami, Mori, and me—for the Seder at Abuela and Abuelo's house. There we were joined by Papi's younger sister, Fanny, and my uncle and younger cousins, Albertico and Rebequita, who also lived in Canarsie. Upon entering the house, you smelled the olive oil, honey, lemons, and almonds. It was like someone had opened a perfume bottle filled with the memory of Spain. And I'd hear the voices of Abuela and Abuelo speaking that Spanish for which I had no name at the time, but which sounded like a song from long, long ago. Abuela called me Rutica (she was the only one who did) and she'd clasp me in her soft embrace and I'd sink into the fullness of her body. Mami said we had to watch ourselves and not eat too much of her food because we'd grow fat like her if we did, but I didn't care, I wanted to fill my plate over and over with everything she cooked with her warm hands.

Abuela hardly ever left the house. She never worked anywhere but at home, cooking and looking after things. That must have been the women's tradition she brought from Turkey. Abuelo worked in the factory of Goodman's Matzoh, so they ate matzoh, the bread of affliction, all year long. He did all the food shopping, sparing Abuela from having to go out and tire herself carrying packages. Baba would have been miserable living this way, but Abuela was content. One grandmother wanted to be enmeshed in the world; the other grandmother wanted to be solitary and stand apart from it. I could see myself in both of them. There was the part of me that wanted to travel and go places and there was the part of me that wanted to be quiet at my desk, thinking and writing.

Unlike Baba, who cooked for special occasions, Abuela always had delicacies on hand whenever we happened to stop in. And for Passover, she'd go all out, creating food that seemed very unusual to me from the Ashkenazi perspective. The hard-boiled eggs, including the one on the Seder Plate, were boiled and roasted for many hours with onion peels, and they were the first thing we ate after we finished reading the Haggadah. Then the feast began in earnest. There were grape leaves stuffed with pine nuts and leek-and-walnut fritters. The egg-lemon soup was tangy and comforting, and the green beans cooked with ripe tomatoes were so wonderful you forgot they were vegetables. The sautéed chicken, breaded lightly with matzoh meal, melted in your mouth, and the potatoes and peppers roasted in the oven were heavenly. All the food swam in olive oil. That, Mami said, was what made it taste so good and also made it so fattening.

For dessert, there was rose petal jam to spread on matzoh. Who knew jam could be made out of flowers? There were Turkish delights and Spanish turrón. But the queen of all the desserts that Abuela offered us was the tishpishti. This was a cake made of crushed almonds and honey that had slowly soaked up a sugary syrup that dripped over your fingers and tasted of happiness.

Abuelo led the Seder, moving between Hebrew, Ladino, and Spanish. He loved to sing, and he sang proudly. After the four of us kids—my brother and me and Albertico and Rebequita—chanted the Four Questions, he sang them in Ladino. When we got to Dayenu, we kids sang it in Hebrew, and he sang the song again in Ladino and it sounded beautiful:

Si rasgava a nos a la mar, i non mos aziya pasar entre eya por lo seko, mos abastava.
Had He split the Sea for us, and not led us through it on dry land, Dayenu.

In the Sephardic tradition, the Afikomen isn't hidden right away. It is passed around to each person seated at the

Seder table and you carry it, or balance it, on your shoulder for a few minutes as the Haggadah is being read. Each person has to imagine and feel what it was like to be enslaved and weighed down by bricks and mortar. I'd watch as everyone took turns carrying the bundle of the afikomen, looking so serious, being careful not to let the afikomen fall. That's when I knew we were really *reliving* the memory of not being free. Once the afikomen had circulated around the table, then Abuelo would hide it.

Abuela made the haroset out of chopped raisins and almonds to create a thick, sweet paste. It was delicious. Later on, I learned you could add dates and dried apricots to the mix, too, but Abuela's haroset was sublime. When it came time for the Korech, Abuelo would make "sandwichitos" for each of us at the table, with matzoh and the haroset and the bitter herb, which was a gentle leaf of romaine lettuce that tasted a lot better than the horseradish. All of us, with our korech in hand, then followed Abuelo's lead as he dramatically leaned to the left when we bit into this sandwich of sandwiches. It was the prized "sandwichito." The raisin haroset was mortar to enjoy! We kids would ask for seconds and thirds. Then it was time to eat the hard-boiled eggs and devour all of Abuela's wonderful food.

There were more songs to sing before we could leave the table. I remember we sang the Ladino version of En Kelohenu:

En Kelohenu, en kadonenu, en k'malkenu, en k'moshienu.
Non como muestro Dyo, non como muestro senyor, non komo
muestro rey, non komo muestro Salvador.

We kids would go searching for the afikomen, and when we found it, we were rewarded with a big smile from Abuelo, who then would bring us back to the table to sing another song:

Bendigamos al Altissimo,
al Sinyor que nos crio.
Demosle agradecimiento
por los bienes que nos Dio.

Bless the Highest One
the Lord who raised us.
Show him our gratitude
for all that he has given us.

The songs would echo inside me as we drove back to Queens in the dark of night. I wish there had been cell phones back then and I could have recorded them. I wish I could hear the voice of Abuelo singing again. And I wish I could eat Abuela's tishpishti again. Theirs was the second Seder, but it was magical, because it showed me that the world is filled with possibilities. The Seder didn't have to be one way; it could be another way and still be a Seder, still be a meal where we remembered the journey to freedom and the dream of home.

Today, many years later, a revitalization of Sephardic music and culture is taking place. Courses in Ladino are available to all who fear this endangered language will be lost. Similarly, many are learning Yiddish in university classes and at the Yiddish Book Center (and the language also thrives among Orthodox Jews). There is a movement to revive the traditions of Yiddishkeit, whether through klezmer music or Yiddish presentations of *Fiddler on the Roof*. I am glad for these efforts at cultural preservation and have participated in them myself.

Still, I wish I'd paid closer attention to these cultures when I was young. Back then, I felt sandwiched between the traditions of my Ashkenazi and Sephardic grandparents, between different foods, languages, memories. I didn't want to have to choose between them; I wanted them all to be part of me. What I couldn't know was how much I'd miss those days of my youth when I witnessed two cultures in all their wholeness, so perfectly alive, in the two Seders.

Now I am a grandmother. As my two little granddaughters grow, I will have to find ways to share with them the love I felt for both sets of grandparents, the joy I found in the two Seders, and the beauty of the different traditions that were passed on to me. I speak neither Yiddish nor Ladino, though

I know a few words of each. I'm not much of a cook, though I can make a nice tishpishti and my matzoh balls from the mix are pretty good. I have a feeling that what I'll be passing on at my Seders will be the stories. All I can hope is that my *nietecitas* will carry them forward.

> ᘛᘏᘘ

Back when I was young, after the two Seders, we would observe Passover at home. Mami wanted to sweeten the days when we couldn't eat bread and she'd make *frituritas*, crispy fritters with matzoh and egg that Mori and I were allowed to smother with big spoonfuls of sugar. And she gave us thick slices of guava and cheese on matzoh, a special Cuban Passover treat.

At last, Passover would end, and it was time to celebrate. Mami and Papi and the group of their Jewish Cuban friends would organize an outing to their favorite Cuban restaurant. Off we'd go, El Grupo and all the El Grupo kids, twenty-five or more of us, to El Rincon Criollo. This hole-in-the-wall restaurant prepared the best Cuban food in New York, and they had a jukebox, too. Warm slices of Cuban bread came out first, and we devoured them. Bread again! Hallelujah! Then came the plates of black beans and rice. How we'd missed the best comfort food of the Cuban diet! We didn't have pork out of respect for our Jewish traditions, but chicken and steak and fish were OK. And there were fried plantains and the yucca covered in garlic sauce that only Cubans know how to appreciate. How lucky we were when René, the owner, brought out for dessert the plates of dulce de coco that everyone yearned for, the grated coconut in syrup that made you feel like you were sitting under a palm tree and you'd never left Cuba . . . even as the rattle of the train shook the walls. And then René would turn on the jukebox and we'd listen:

Cuando salí de Cuba
Dejé mi vida, dejé mi amor
Cuando salí de Cuba
Dejé enterrado mi corazón

When I left Cuba
I left my life, I left my love
When I left Cuba
I left my heart buried there

I watched as Mami and Papi and their friends sang along wistfully, and I thought about how all the different identities came together in me—Jewish, Cuban, Ashkenazi, Sephardic, and American—and how I was the sum total of all these lives and journeys. I was sandwiched between identities and between all the flavors I had been blessed to taste and remember.

SHULCHAN ORECH

Finally. The main meal. There are no specific instructions on what to eat, giving families the freedom to prepare the meal however they like or according to their specific traditions. Ashkenazi Jews—whose families have certain roots in Europe—might enjoy matzah ball soup, gefilte fish, maybe brisket. Sephardi or Mizrahi Jews—whose families have roots in Spain, the Middle East, or North Africa—might enjoy dishes with fava beans, stews, maybe slow-cooked tomatoes and peppers. There is no *one* Jewish food tradition; and there might be as many different meals on the first night of Passover as there are Seders in the world.

- *There are lots of ways to celebrate a holiday, lots of ways to remember. Why do you think so many holidays are centered around sitting at a table and eating a meal?*

- *Why do you think it takes so long to reach this point? If you were creating the steps of the Seder from scratch, where would you put the meal?*

- *If you could host a meal with anyone who has ever lived, who would you invite and why? If you could host a meal with anyone who hasn't lived—any fictional characters ever created—who would you invite and why?*

- *What are some of your favorite foods? What are some of your least favorite foods? Have you ever been to a meal where they were served? What happened next?*

WHY I HATE GEFILTE FISH

BY SARAH KAPIT

I can smell the gefilte fish even before Grandma brings it out from the kitchen. And let me tell you: it is G-R-O-S-S. The grossest.

I hate, and I mean *hate*, gefilte fish. I once wrote an entire list about it.

TOP 3 REASONS WHY GEFILTE FISH IS GROSS AND NOT FIT FOR HUMAN CONSUMPTION
by Myra Pribeagu

1. The color. It's just so gray and so ugly. Who wants to eat something that shares a color with throw up? Not me!
2. The texture. Lots of foods have textures that I don't like, but gefilte fish is the worst. The very sight of those tiny bumps sticking out from the fish makes my skin crawl. When I think about actually putting that in my mouth…just no. No, no, and no.
3. The smell. That's quite possibly the worst thing about gefilte fish. It's even worse than you'd expect from a dead fish. I guess when all the dead fishy smell has been stewing in a jar for weeks, it just keeps getting smellier. I can't stand it. I really can't.

And now, that awful smell has been unleashed on the dining room.

I've tried to be good during this Seder. I really, really have. Mom gave me a squishy ball to use as a fidget before the Seder began. While everyone reads from the haggadah, I've been squishing the ball. It feels good to grip in my hands, making it easier for me to sit in place. Aunt Becca started to say something about it, but Mom told her to be quiet. According to Mom, I am allowed to play with squishy balls at the dinner table. They help me. Especially when dinner is a Seder that goes on forever and ever and ever.

Thanks to my squishy ball, I get through most of the Seder OK. Now is the good part, the part where we eat. At least, this is supposed to be the good part. Maybe it would be . . . except for the gefilte fish.

Aunt Becca comes around the table with the gefilte fish platter in hand. With every step she takes, the horrible smell gets stronger and stronger and I can't concentrate on anything else. She ladles a grayish lump onto every plate. Whenever I look at it, a shiver runs through my body.

How can anyone possibly eat this stuff?

Too soon, Aunt Becca is standing right over me. I can tell what she's going to do before it happens.

"No! No, no, no!" I say.

Maybe I'm being a little rude, but Aunt Becca is breaking a rule. At my house, we always pass around the food plates. No one has to take anything they don't want. Here at Grandma's house, at the Seder, all the rules are different. I do not like that one single bit.

"Don't be ridiculous, Myra," Aunt Becca says. "This is your grandmother's world-famous gefilte fish. She worked for hours to give you this meal. The least you can do is give it a try."

My neck starts to get very, very hot.

"But I don't like gefilte fish! I know I don't like it."

"You don't like store-bought gefilte fish, maybe. This is different," Aunt Becca proclaims. "This is the best gefilte fish there is."

"I don't care. I don't like it."

"How can you possibly know that when you haven't even tried it?"

I cross my arms. "I *know*. I won't eat it!"

Aunt Becca purses her lips. "You're twelve years old! Some girls are bat mitzvahs at your age. You're far too old to be making a fuss like this."

She shoots a look at Mom. I know that look. I've seen it before—not just on Aunt Becca's frowny face but on Uncle Adam's, too. I've seen it in random people who walk past us in restaurants. I've seen it from more than one teacher. I've even seen Grandma make that face.

The why-are-you-like-this face. Why can't you be like everyone else, Myra? Why do you always have to make such a fuss about everything? Why can't you just *be normal*?

The thing is, I'm not normal and I'm not like everyone else. I'm autistic. That means a lot of things, but for me one of the biggest is that I'm really sensitive to certain sensory things. Like the sound of a roaring motorcycle or the feeling of an itchy shirt tag scratching against my neck.

Or the taste of smelly, awful, no-good gefilte fish.

Everyone in the family knows I'm autistic. But that doesn't mean they understand.

"Becca . . ." Mom says. "This doesn't have to be a big thing. Myra can eat what she likes."

A warm glow spreads through me. Mom defended me! Just like she always does.

Still, a part of me wishes that I could defend myself. But I don't know how.

I try to clear my head and focus on what's important: the food. Using my fork, I separate the yucky gefilte fish from the rest of my meal. I'm extra-careful to make sure none of the gross gefilte juice seeps over to the chicken and potatoes. Chicken and potatoes are on my good-to-eat list. But not if they get contaminated by the gefilte juice.

I pick up a chicken leg and chew. I try to enjoy it, I really do, but . . . the gefilte smell is still right there. Overpowering the yummy taste of the chicken.

Ugh!

I place down the chicken leg. There has to be a way out of this. I just don't know what.

"Myra-medele?"

I glance up at Grandma. She smiles at me in that Grandma way of hers, eyes warm and crinkly.

"Aren't you going to give the gefilte fish a try?"

I want to say yes. I want to make Grandma happy. But the fish . . . the smell . . . the everything. She doesn't understand.

"Just give it a try," Grandma says. "One bite, medele?"

For some reason, this is important to her. Like, really, really important. I don't know why, but it is. And I don't want to hurt Grandma's feelings, not if I can help it.

I wish I could explain everything to her better, but I just can't.

Well, I guess I can manage one bite. It shouldn't be a big deal, right?

I stab my fork into the gefilte fish and make a tiny slice. OK, I can do this. Closing my eyes, I lift the fork to my mouth and begin to chew.

The moment the taste of it hits my tongue, I want to spit it back out. So I do.

Now everyone is looking at me. I can't blame them. The whole thing is totally gross, even grosser than normal gefilte fish. My face is on fire.

"You really couldn't finish a bite?" Grandma asks softly.

I'm not always the best at understanding faces and voices, but I'm pretty sure that Grandma is disappointed. In me.

Tears start to overflow my eyes, too fast and too hard.

"Medele?" Grandma asks. "What's wrong?"

I don't respond. Can't.

Aunt Becca points a finger at Mom. "You indulge her too much, Leah. Why can't she eat like everyone else?"

I don't wait for Mom's response. All I know is that I need to get out out out now now can't wait everything bad.

Shove my plate to the side. Get up. Leave table.

Too fast. My glass of grape juice falls to the ground. *Clang.* Juice splatters on my shirt. Grapey liquid everywhere, in my nose and on my face. People make loud sounds, angry sounds too loud too angry too much no good can't can't can't make it stop please please please

I run.

I escape. I make it to Mom and Aunt Becca's old bedroom. When I visit Grandma, this is where I sleep. It's the closest thing to a private place in Grandma's small house.

Immediately, I throw myself on the bed. It creaks a little and I flinch.

Even though the room is empty, I am surrounded by people. There are at least a dozen photos of me and my cousins, plus Mom and Aunt Becca when they were kids. I am being watched by a bajillion eyeballs.

At least these versions of my family can't talk to me. They can't tell me that I'm bad. They can't make me eat gefilte fish.

"I'm not even hungry anymore," I say to the room of photos. "I can stay in here for hours. No problem."

But just then my stomach rumbles, exposing me for the liar that I am. I roll over onto my stomach and squeeze my eyes shut. How did everything turn so very wrong? All because of some yucky, awful, no-good gefilte fish?

Why can't everyone just let me *be*?

If there was a way to get out of here without ever having to see Grandma and Aunt Becca and everyone else, I would take it. But there isn't. Even if I wanted to try escaping through the window, I know for a fact that it doesn't open. The last time I stayed overnight, I tried it. I'm stuck.

Sooner or later, I will have to leave this room. I'll have to face everyone.

I'll have to deal with the awful fishy gefilte-smell.

As I bounce on the bed, I try to count to one hundred in my head. Sometimes that helps me calm down. But counting reminds me of the part in the Seder when we count, one of the parts that's still coming up. And I don't want to think about the stupid Seder right now. I want to go home.

Someone knocks on the door.

"I'm not here!" I yell.

"OK, Myra-who-is-not-here," Mom says. "I'll go back downstairs. But if you do decide to come back and you want to talk, text me."

The footsteps go away and I am alone again. But it doesn't come as a relief.

I sigh. Mom is trying to help. I know that. So I take out my cell phone and text her.

You can come.

She joins me on the bed a few minutes later. "Hi," she says.

"Hi," I mumble.

"How are you doing?"

Sometimes, Mom asks really obvious questions. It's a grown-up thing, I guess.

I scowl. "Not good!"

Mom holds up a hand. "Yeah, I know. Think deeper, Myra-la. If you can identify the specific emotions you're feeling, we can work to make things better. Are you angry? Scared? Stressed out?"

I think about it. Before, when everything happened, my face was on fire and my head was going to explode. I was mad. Really, really mad. But now all that's gone. I just feel tired. Empty. I want to crawl under the covers. If I could, I'd stay in bed until tomorrow morning. Maybe by then every-thing would magically be better.

"I was angry, but . . . I don't know. Now I'm just . . . sad?"

Mom nods. "It's OK to be sad. What happened is a lot."

"But it's Passover!"

"That doesn't mean you can't be sad."

OK, so I am sad and I know it. But that doesn't really solve the problem.

"I'm hungry," I admit. "But I can't go back to Grandma and Aunt Becca and everyone!"

Sighing, Mom runs a hand through her curly hair. "If you want, I can bring you some food to eat here."

I imagine myself eating chicken and potatoes and matzo kugel alone in the bedroom. I don't hate the idea. It would be easy, probably. Easier than going back to the Seder.

But sooner or later I'll have to go back, won't I? I'll have to face the rest of the family. I can't avoid them forever, even if I want to. (And right now I sort of do.)

I close my eyes. I take deep breaths. One, two, three. Then I open my eyes.

"I'll go back."

Mom squeezes my hand.

～～～

I hold my breath as I go back to the Seder. I know, I just *know*, that everyone has been talking about me. That they will all be looking at me, demanding answers.

Only they don't look my way at all. My family is busy with all the usual dinner things—talking and laughing and eating. My little cousin Danny is focused on arranging his peas into a smiley face.

No one gives me more than a passing glance.

Someone has cleaned up the grape juice I spilled, and an

empty plate is waiting for me by my spot. There's still plenty of food left, even now.

The gefilte fish platter sits at the other end of the table. I try not to look at it. I help myself to non-gefilte fish food and start digging in.

Grandma smiles at me. "It's good to see you again, medele."

I want to tell her that I'm glad to see her, too, but my mouth is full of matzo kugel. And anyway, I'm not sure that it's true. Seeing Grandma and Aunt Becca and everyone . . . well, some of the bad feelings are coming back to me. My skin feels all tingly, and my eyes sting. But I will not cry. I won't.

It doesn't help that the gefilte smell is still here, invading my space once again. I try to ignore the smell, but it's hard. Everything is hard.

"Grandma," I start to talk, then stop. I don't know what to say. I don't want to hurt her feelings, but . . .

"Do you need something?" she asks.

Deep breaths—one, two, three.

"Yes." I try to give myself courage. I have the right to ask this question. Even if Aunt Becca and everyone else thinks I'm being difficult. "If everyone's done with the gefilte fish, could we maybe put it back into the kitchen? The smell . . . it's kind of hard for me. Because of sensory stuff."

She twists her face into an expression I don't quite understand. But I don't think she's mad at me. At least I hope she isn't mad at me.

"Sensory stuff," she repeats. "Can you explain what that means?"

My tongue feels heavy, and the awful gefilte-smell is still swirling around me. But I try to explain.

"It's an autism thing. Sometimes, sounds and sights and smells are just . . . too much for me," I say.

She nods. "All right, then. I'm sorry I wasn't more understanding earlier."

She pats me on the shoulder in just the way I like—firm touch, not light. Then she asks Uncle Adam to take the gefilte fish away.

The smell is gone, and I can breathe again.

"Thanks," I whisper to Grandma. "I really do like the chicken."

Her face relaxes into a big, big smile.

"Anything for my medele. You just have to tell me what you need." She winks. "And you're very welcome for the chicken."

I glance over at Aunt Becca. Did she hear everything I said? I hope that she did, but it's hard to tell. She's busy telling Danny not to throw his peas, for goodness' sake.

Maybe my aunt doesn't understand why I don't like gefilte fish. Maybe she never will. I don't know. But Grandma understands. Because I told her.

For now, that's enough.

I return to my plate and I start to eat.

TZAFUN

The story has been told. The meal is over. And now, in this step of the Seder, the afikoman is eaten. Remember step four: Yachatz, when a bit of matzah was put aside for later. For many families, that bit was *hidden* (which is what the word "Tzafun" means in Hebrew) and now is found, often by kids searching in hopes of winning a prize. The afikoman is then broken up into smaller pieces, passed around the table, and shared. By tradition, it's the last thing eaten around the Seder table. In fact, the word "afikoman" might stem from an ancient Greek word for "dessert."

- *Have you ever found something that was lost?*

- *Why do you think the afikoman is the final thing eaten at the Seder?*

- *For many families, finding the afikoman becomes a little game of matzah hide-and-seek. Does your family play games during any holiday? Can you invent a game, for Passover or any other occasion?*

- *Lots of things can be hidden: a bit of food, an object, even pieces of ourselves. Have you ever shared something about yourself that you'd previously kept hidden?*

THE AWFUL OMEN

BY A. J. SASS

Sammy's phone buzzed nonstop on the drive from Chicago to their grandparents' house in Michigan's Upper Peninsula. Most were texts from their cousins' group chat, things like arrival-time updates and guesses about what foods Uncle Seth and his husband, Danny, would be making for the Passover meal later that night.

No big deal. Nothing to stress about.

But Sammy's chest clenched. Each message reminded them of how little time they had left before they came out to their family as nonbinary tonight.

Sammy had thought long and hard about the best time to share their identity and new pronouns. Their family lived all over the Midwest and only ever really came together once a year, for Passover. If Sammy didn't come out tonight, they'd have to wait another whole year—or tell everyone individually, which was *a lot* of coming out.

It had to be tonight. That was why Sammy had created a script and practiced every word until they'd completely memorized it.

A strand of Sammy's long, brown hair slipped out from under their CHICAGO SKY hat. As they tucked it back in, they silently rehearsed their script again:

Hi, everyone. Pesach sameach. I have something important to tell you: I'm nonbinary. Use they, them, and their pronouns for me now, please and thanks.

But just thinking about everyone staring at them while they explained what "nonbinary" meant made Sammy feel sick. The more they recited the words in their head, the sweatier their palms got and the more their chest clenched. It felt like all the oxygen had been sucked out of the car, leaving Sammy struggling for breath.

Sammy stared out the window and looked for familiar landmarks, trying to distract themself. They weren't nervous about their family accepting them. Not really. Uncle Seth had introduced everyone to Danny a few years ago, back when Danny was his boyfriend instead of his husband, and Sammy's parents had even taken them to a local Pride parade last summer.

The nerves were about something different, something Sammy had struggled with for as long as they could remember. Whenever they had to speak in front of anyone—or even just thought about speaking—their throat closed up and they felt dizzy, making it almost impossible to talk to anyone.

That included relatives. At family gatherings, Sammy's thirteen-year-old cousin, Ava, always led the conversation among their cousins. She was part of a children's theater group and never seemed shy about anything. Sammy's twin cousins, Yael and Ido, would chime in a lot, too. At nine, Caleb was the youngest and could be counted on to say something silly, which always made Ido laugh and Ava and Yael roll their eyes.

Sammy would listen but stay quiet, unless someone spoke to them directly.

"Not far now," Mom called from the front seat as Dad hummed along to the radio.

Sammy glanced up in time to see their car roll past a big blue sign welcoming visitors to PURE MICHIGAN. They looked back at their phone, and their eyes snagged on a mention of Uncle Seth in the cousins' group chat. In that moment, it occurred to Sammy that maybe they could come out to Uncle Seth first and ask him to share the news with everyone else. That didn't sound too scary.

Sammy quickly dismissed the idea. Their uncle would be busy making dinner and leading the Seder. Plus, just because Uncle Seth was married to a man didn't mean he'd automatically understand what being nonbinary meant. And if Uncle Seth didn't fully get it, he wouldn't be able to answer questions from Sammy's other relatives, who definitely knew less than he did. Sammy would have to step in and explain, which wasn't any better than reciting their script in the first place.

Sammy's phone blinked with a new message from Ava: *The afikomen is mine again, I'm calling it now!!*

It was another reminder about tonight. Even though searching for the afikomen was one of Sammy's favorite parts of the Seder, dread pooled in their stomach when they thought about speaking to their family after.

In Sammy's family, finding the afikomen came with a perk: a prize of the winner's choosing. Ava was an expert at locating the afikomen; she found it every year. And every year, the rest of the cousins sent a flood of texts claiming this Seder would be different.

Yael said, *lololol not happening.*

Ido followed with, *it's my year to find it!*

Caleb sent a GIF of a turtle that was stuck upside down on its shell. It used its own momentum to right itself as text flashed: CHALLENGE ACCEPTED.

Sammy's thumbs hovered over their phone, planning a reply of their own, but they weren't even sure they'd be happy if they found the afikomen this year. Because then they'd have to figure out a prize to ask for when all they truly wanted was to come out as nonbinary without having to answer a million questions.

Wait a sec.

Sammy blinked, barely aware that Dad had turned onto their grandparents' street.

What if I could combine those two things?

Because their family had never refused a *reasonable* request. The only time the adults had made anyone pick again was when Ava had asked for a pet horse when she was six, probably because she and Aunt Sarah lived in an apartment that didn't have a backyard. (Plus, horses were expensive.)

But. *But!* If Sammy found the afikomen first, they could ask Uncle Seth to tell everyone to start using they, them, and their pronouns for them, full stop. No questions allowed. That felt like a reasonable request their family would have to accept.

Ava was the single biggest obstacle to Sammy finding the afikomen. But this was really important, so maybe she'd agree to a compromise or something. Sammy switched out of their group chat, messaging Ava directly: *Hey, I really need the afikomen this year*

Or at least that was what Sammy thought they'd typed. When Ava sent back *???*, Sammy looked again.

Their phone had corrected *afikomen* to *awful omen*.

And that made Sammy's chest clench all over again.

It doesn't mean anything, Sammy told themself. *At least, I don't think it—*

"All right, folks, here we are!"

Sammy practically jumped through the sunroof at the sound of Dad's voice. Sure enough, they'd come to a stop in front of Grandpa and Grandma's house without Sammy noticing. Their pulse raced as they glanced up the long driveway, searching for Ava's mom's car.

Gotta find her, gotta find her.

Sammy tore off toward the house.

"Whoa, where's the fire?" Dad joked.

"Hat off, sweetie," Mom called.

Usually, Sammy hated taking off their hat; it felt like they were removing protective armor. But the sooner they got inside, the sooner they could talk to Ava and convince her to let them find the afikomen. Sammy tugged off their hat, letting their hair tumble down their back.

They rang the bell, eyeing the flurry of movement through the nearest window. Muffled laughter drifted to them. The buzz of conversations. They gripped the rim of their hat between tense fingers.

As the door swung open and Grandma held out her arms to hug them, Sammy tried their best not to think about that autocorrected text.

⁕⁂⁜

As soon as Sammy entered their grandparents' house, Uncle Seth ushered them into the dining room and told them to take a seat at the table. Sammy squirmed in their chair, wedged between Dad on one side and Mom on the other.

Ava was sitting on the complete opposite side of the table, her dark brown hair tied back with a purple ribbon. She and Yael chattered nonstop. Sammy caught words like "production" and "stage" and "makeup" before Grandpa started asking Sammy's thoughts on the latest WNBA player trades.

Normally, Sammy loved talking about their favorite sport, but all they could think about was Ava and the afikomen. They were grateful when Uncle Seth stood up and got things started.

Sammy tried to get Ava's attention during the Kadesh. Ava's gaze paused on them at one point, but then Uncle Seth passed all the kids glasses of grape juice, and Yael whispered something to Ava. She didn't look back over at Sammy.

Then, when everyone lined up to wash their hands, Sammy tried to inch closer to Ava. But that only caused Ido and Yael's dad, Sammy's Uncle Ran, to pat their back and say, "Wait your turn, kid," with a fake-stern expression.

Ava looked back at Sammy then, but only for a second.

Awful omen.

Sammy swallowed hard over the lump in their throat.

By the time Uncle Seth broke the matzah and slid one piece inside the familiar blue drawstring bag, Sammy's legs were bouncing uncontrollably under the table. They watched Uncle Seth pass the afikomen to Grandma. She winked at the kids as she stood, then headed out of the room.

Sammy had never wanted to run after someone so badly.

But first, they had more of the Seder to get through.

Usually, Sammy loved each part of the Seder. This year was also special, because for the very first time, Uncle Seth had cooked the dinner with the help of Danny, who was a professional chef. On top of the matzo ball soup and bris-ket and gefilte fish Sammy's family ate every year, the uncles revealed they would also be serving new dishes, like honey-crunch matzo brittle and vanilla noodle kugel.

Mouth-watering scents drifted from the kitchen, but Sammy hardly noticed them. By the time Grandma returned, all Sammy could think about was where she had hidden the afikomen.

Sammy looked over at Ava again as Caleb stood to ask the Four Questions. She seemed to be studying Grandma, prob-ably strategizing where to search first.

Awful omen.

Sammy's pulse quickened.

The Four Questions came and went. Everyone washed their hands again and listened to another blessing. Then din-ner was served. Uncle Seth's and Danny's smiles widened with every compliment.

Sammy hardly processed any of it.

Finally—*finally*—Uncle Seth stood and cleared his throat.

"Our more solemn memories of enslavement are balanced by the playfulness associated with finding the afikomen," he said. "It's meant to be a joyful celebration of freedom—and, of course, it comes with a coveted prize for whoever locates it. So, push back your chairs and start your engines. The time to search for the afikomen starts . . . now!"

The kids shot out of their seats and darted into the family room. Yael and Ido worked as a team, Ido lifting chair cushions and Yael putting them back in place. Caleb peered inside the back of the grand piano at one end of the room, while Ava searched through drawers in Grandma's antique desk in the opposite corner.

Sammy knew they needed to talk to Ava, but in the excitement of the moment, they couldn't help stopping at the fireplace to peek behind the framed photos on the mantle. By the time they looked up, Ava wasn't at Grandma's desk anymore.

She wasn't in the room at all.

Panic fluttered in Sammy's stomach. They looked around, but Yael, Ido, and Caleb seemed oblivious to Ava's disappearance. Caleb dashed toward the staircase. Every step creaked as he made his way upstairs. If Ava had gone in the same direction, Sammy was positive they'd have heard it.

They headed back into the dining room instead, where the adults were chatting. The conversation stopped as all eyes shifted toward them, and Sammy couldn't help imagining what it would be like for them later that night if Ava found the afikomen.

Their throat tightened. They had to find it first. There was no other option.

Sammy sprinted out of the room fast, into the kitchen. The sound of their relatives' chuckles followed them.

Ava wasn't in the kitchen or the downstairs bathroom. Sammy stopped in front of the coat rack, eyes snagging on their CHICAGO SKY hat. Their fingers itched to put it back on and hide from the world, but their eyes caught a flash of purple outside the nearest window. They peered at a big bush that grew along the side of the house. On summer visits, Sammy would help Grandma pick raspberries off it. Right now, in late April, it was mostly just a prickly bush with a few leaves sprouting here and there.

On a hunch, they opened the door and sprinted out into the yard.

Ava stood at the far end of the raspberry bush. Her purple ribbon fluttered in the wind. Sammy's gaze landed on it, then lowered to Ava's hand.

Her fingers grabbed a small object, but Sammy could still make out the rich, velvety blue fabric.

Awful omen.

Their heart sank as they made their way over to her.

Ava looked back at Sammy with a satisfied smile. "I told everyone I'd find it again this year."

Sammy swallowed. "How'd you even know it'd be out here? She's never hidden it outside the house before."

"It wasn't really that hard." She shrugged. "Grandma always hides it in things that are special to her: the potpourri basket Great Aunt Esther gave her, her favorite mug, stuff like that. She loves writing letters and making raspberry jam, too, so when it wasn't in her desk, I figured it had to be out here."

Sammy looked down at their feet.

"It's perfect timing, too," Ava continued. "I've been saving up for a sewing machine so I can help make costumes for my theater club, but they can be *super* expensive."

The longer Sammy stood next to Ava, the harder their pulse pounded. Their plan had utterly failed. They still had their script, sure. They could still recite it for everyone later. But the more Sammy thought about it, the hotter their body felt. Deep down, they knew they were going to chicken out.

"I really needed to find it this year," they whispered.

"Your birthday's not that far away. Just ask for what you want then."

"I can't wait that long." Sammy glanced up. "Unless—I mean, could you maybe say I found it?"

Ava studied them. "Why would I—"

Before she could finish, the house door flew open. Caleb scampered into the yard, with Yael and Ido close behind.

Caleb spotted the afikomen in Ava's hand, then groaned.

"Noooo. She found it *again*."

"Yep," Ava said. "But Sammy just asked if I could let them say they found it."

Except Ava didn't say "them" or "they" when referring to Sammy. She used pronouns that felt like the itchy dress socks Sammy's parents insisted they wear at their temple on Shabbat. Sammy cringed, but no one seemed to notice.

Yael pointed at Sammy. "They aren't the only one who wants to win."

But Yael didn't use the right pronoun, either. Sammy's throat got tighter and tighter.

"Give it to me instead!" Caleb bounced up and down.

Suddenly, everyone was talking at once, trying to convince Ava to give them the afikomen.

Everyone but Sammy, who felt like they were a rubber band pulled farther than it could withstand.

"Use *they*!" Sammy snapped.

Their cousins went quiet.

"What?" Ava tilted her head, nose scrunched up.

Sammy swallowed but made themself explain.

"You were saying the wrong pronouns," they told Ava and Yael. "I use *they*, *them*, and *their* now. I'm . . . nonbinary."

"Oh my gosh." Yael's eyes widened. "I'm so sorry. I didn't know."

"Wait, wait, what does *nonbinary* mean?" Caleb asked, still bouncing.

"It means someone who isn't a boy or a girl," Ava said. "One of my theater friends is gender-fluid. That's similar, right?"

Sammy nodded but still couldn't look her in the eye. "That's why I really needed to find the afikomen tonight."

"OK, but," Ido jumped in, "what does the afikomen have to do with you being, um . . ."

"Nonbinary," Yael said.

"Yeah," Caleb shouted. "What does it have to do with that?"

Ava raised her hand, and the rest of Sammy's cousins quieted down again.

"I wanted to find the afikomen so I could ask everyone to start using the right pronouns for me," Sammy explained. "I thought if I chose that as my prize, they'd have to say yes and then I wouldn't have to answer all their questions."

"You don't want to answer questions about who you are?" Ava asked.

"Yeah. I mean, no. It's not that." Suddenly, all Sammy's worries flooded out. "I get really nervous having to talk in front of people. Like, the I-feel-like-puking kind of nervous. The less I have to talk, the better."

For a moment, Sammy hung their head. "I know it's ridiculous. I just feel so—"

"Actually," Ava cut in, "I get nervous having to talk in front of people, too."

Sammy looked at her. "You do?"

"You bet. Why do you think I help with my theater club's makeup and want to learn to sew costumes? That stuff is fun, obviously, but it also lets me feel like I'm part of the show without having to be onstage with everyone staring at me."

Sammy hadn't considered that before.

"I get super nervous during school presentations," Yael said.

"Yeah, same." Ido nodded.

"One time, I threw up all over my math book right before a big test." Caleb looked solemn. "But then I found out I had the flu."

Ido laughed, and Ava and Yael rolled their eyes. A smile tugged at the corners of Sammy's mouth. But then they thought about reciting their script in front of the adults again, and it dissolved.

"I just wish I didn't have to do this alone," they whispered. "I'm a lot better at group projects."

"What if it could be one?"

Sammy looked over at Ava. "What do you mean?

"Like, what if we all stand with you? So you're not alone." She glanced at the others. "We could do that, right?"

They all nodded. Ava looked back at Sammy expectantly.

Sammy imagined standing alone in front of all their relatives again. Their chest still clenched, but it relaxed the moment they imagined Ava, Yael, Ido, and Caleb beside them.

"I think that would work," they said.

"Cool!" Caleb said. "I'll go tell everyone you have a Very Important Announcement."

Yael and Ido shared a look as Caleb darted back toward the house. "We'll go make sure he doesn't spoil anything before you can share it," Yael said.

As soon as the twins were gone, Ava pulled out her phone. She flashed Sammy's last text at them with a grin. "Guess today wasn't such an 'awful omen,' after all, huh?"

"I guess not." Sammy continued to think about this as they entered the house, passed through the kitchen, and paused at the entrance to the dining room. The nerves were still there, but they felt a little easier to accept now that they'd survived coming out to their cousins. They were just a part of who Sammy was, like being nonbinary and Jewish.

"You ready for this?" Ava asked.

This time when Sammy's stomach fluttered at the thought of talking to their relatives, it felt less scary, more exciting. It felt like watching the Chicago Sky win their first-ever championship in the WNBA Final and the wonderful, swooping sensation they'd felt when they first realized they were nonbinary.

"Yeah, I'm ready." Sammy took a calming breath, then entered the dining room with Ava.

BARECH

Third to last step: Barech, which means "blessing." Grace after the meal. Followed by another mysterious ritual: Many reach this step and send someone from the table to open the door. By tradition, the Seder table is then visited by an invisible guest—the prophet Elijah—who even has his own cup of wine or grape juice set on the table. Why does Elijah "visit"? Maybe because, in the stories about him, he's often there to lend a helping hand. Or maybe because, in other stories, his efforts fail, he loses hope—and this ritual isn't about us wanting comfort *from* Elijah but offering it *to* him. Showing him a table of friends and family, eating together, celebrating together, with love.

- *Like many parts of the Seder, the traditional "Barech" step is long. There might be folks who are uncomfortable with the words, who might be unfamiliar with them. Have you ever been somewhere you felt out of place? Did anyone make you feel more comfortable? How? Have you ever seen someone else feel out of place? Did you make them feel comfortable? How?*

- *One of the lines said in this step is, "I have never seen a good person suffer." Is this true? If not, why say it?*

- *Barech is one of many steps of the Seder that some families might sing. Are there any songs you connect to moments from your life? Songs that—anytime you hear them—make you remember some moment, some person, some feeling?*

- *Many Passover traditions—including the Seder—have changed over time. Does your family have any tradition you wish you could change? How would you change it?*

MUSIC AND MATZO

BY LAURA SHOVAN

In Hebrew, instead of "Once upon a time," we say *Hayoh hayah* when we're about to tell a story. I love how musical those words sound. Or maybe they just remind me of my name, Hannah.

I have a story to tell. A story with fighting and snakes, floods and escapes, music and matzo. *Hayoh hayah.*

❧

My family was getting ready for our Seder. My brothers, Raffi and Jared; our parents; and I had spent the entire weekend scouring the house. It's one of the things I love about the Passover festival—spring cleaning is built right in. And so is singing.

It was spring break. Ms. Krulik, my chorus teacher, wanted me to try out for honors chorale on our first day back at school. Time was running out to pick an audition song.

I wanted to be a singer someday. Maybe I'd finally convince my parents to let me take voice lessons and audition at our local theater. Or maybe, when I was older, I'd study to become a cantor at a synagogue. Singing was my favorite thing about school, about family gatherings, about going to services, about everything! I'd spent days listening to a Spotify channel called "Classic Ballads," but they were all boring love songs. Broadway tunes from shows like *Oliver!* were no better. Who wanted to sing about how much some guy needed me? Blech! I was holding out for something special, something that made my heart sing along with my voice.

A few days before Passover, I had another solo on my mind: the Four Questions. They're usually sung by the youngest person at the table, but my little brothers and cousins could barely read, let alone memorize a song in Hebrew. My Seder solo was safe for now.

We'd already swapped our everyday plates for the paper ones we'd use over the next week.

"Time to unwrap the Seder china," Mom said, opening a box of dishes wrapped in newspaper. She smiled. "I'm glad you're old enough to help me."

"And careful enough," I added, throwing a glance at my brothers, who were having a pillow fight with the couch cushions I'd just vacuumed.

Mom passed me a plate with delicate spring flowers circling its edge.

That's when she dropped the news and I almost dropped the plate.

"Aunt Maya says Joon and Tae can't wait to sing the Four Questions with your brothers."

"What? But that's my part," I said.

I was the only girl in the family, four years older than any of the boys. At our Seders, the adults always sat at one end of the table, comparing the Exodus to events in the news. On the other end, my little brothers and cousins goofed around and sprayed matzo crumbs all over the place.

Everyone usually ignored me, until I had a chance to sing. When I chanted the Four Questions, Poppy told the boys, "Quiet down!" and Nana's eyes went misty. Aunt Maya always squeezed my hand and said, "Beautiful, Hannah." Without a role in the Seder, I'd be stuck in between. Not a grown-up. Not a little kid. Nobody.

Mom interrupted my thoughts. "We were hoping you'd teach them how to sing it."

My brother Jared was the youngest, but he'd just turned five. The only thing Jared cared about was wheels. Any kind of wheels. He was obsessed with cars, trucks, trains. I might have been able to teach him "Ma nishtana halailah hazeh"—if I changed the tune of the Four Questions to "The Wheels on the Bus Go Round and Round."

"You've got this, Hannah," Mom said.

I placed the plate carefully at the head of the table, Poppy's spot. He would be leading our Seder. Nana and Poppy were Mom and Aunt Maya's parents. Most years, we had to clear all the furniture out of the family room and squish two long tables together. It was the only way we could fit everyone.

But this year was different. My father's parents were on a senior tour, spending Passover in Israel, and Aunt Maya's family was staying on the West Coast.

While I set the table, Dad tinkered with a laptop so they could all join us virtually.

I sighed. Why did everything have to change?

"I'll give it a try," I told Mom. "It'll be kind of cute to hear their little voices singing."

Aunt Maya's two sons were Joon and Tae, who were seven and five. They had Korean names like their dad, my uncle, Jong-in. They also had a three-foot-long ball python named Bagel. After dinner that night, I video chatted with them all. Before I even had a chance to bring up the Four Questions, Joon announced, "Bagel's coming to the Seder."

Tae jumped in. "We're not allowed to eat bagels during Passover. But Bagel isn't food. He's our snake."

"Some people eat snakes," said Joon.

My aunt was laughing in the background.

"Wait a minute," I said, mentally scrolling back through the conversation. "Did you say your snake is coming to Passover?" It was bad enough the boys would be singing my favorite part. This Seder was turning into a circus.

Joon nodded. "Bagel is part of our family. And also I learned at Hebrew school that Moses and Pharaoh got into this epic fight and Moses's brother Aaron flung a stick . . ."

"His staff," Aunt Maya chimed in.

"And the stick turned into a giant snake and Pharaoh was like, AHHHH!" Joon fell out of his chair. He could be very dramatic for a seven-year-old. Of course, Tae had to fall out of his chair, too.

"I give up," I said.

If the four Klein boys (well, two Kleins and two Klein-Kims) were more interested in staging Moses versus Pharaoh stick battles than they were in the Haggadah, maybe I'd get to sing the Four Questions after all.

Aunt Maya leaned into the screen. "I'm counting on you, Hannah Banana." She smiled, so I almost forgave her for using my old nickname. "I promised the boys that Bagel could come to the Seder and they could tell the story of the staff and the serpent." Then she fake-whispered, "It was the only way I could convince them to do the Four Questions and the Four Sons with Raffi and Jared."

I sat back in my chair. "They're doing the Four Sons, too?"

My aunt tucked her hair under a bandanna. She must've still been cleaning. "There are four of them. And they *are* the sons of the family. It couldn't have been better if we'd planned it." She grinned.

"But what about me?" I said.

My aunt didn't hear me. From the off-screen cries of *Oof!* and *Ouch!*, it was clear that my little cousins were still on the floor, wrestling.

Aunt Maya sighed. "They're never going to sit still long

enough to come up with a script for their skit. And I've still got the fridge to clean out. Would you help them, Hannah? You're such a good writer."

"Sure," I said. How could I say no when my cousins needed me?

Once Aunt Maya picked the boys off the floor and sat them in front of her laptop, I taught Joon and Tae the Four Questions—"Wheels on the Bus"–style. Of course, Jared heard me singing his favorite tune and came running. And Raffi, afraid of being left out, squished himself next to me at the table so he could see what was going on.

Over the next couple of days, I had all four boys ready for their Passover debut. I even asked for their ideas for the Moses versus Pharaoh skit, which were mostly about throwing stuff and falling down. I gave the biggest speaking role to the narrator—me. I was going to have a special part at this Seder after all.

That night, Mom came into my room before bedtime. "Tomorrow's the big day," she said.

"I guess."

She plunked down on my bed and slumped against the wall. She must've been extra tired. "What's with the grumpy face? You love Passover, Hannah. It's your favorite holiday."

"Was," I grumbled. "I haven't even had my bat mitzvah, but you all expect me to act like an adult. Teaching the boys the Four Questions. Writing a script for their stupid snake stick battle. And Aunt Maya says they're doing the Four Sons, too."

"But you'll be reading and saying prayers. We take turns so we're all part of the Seder story. That's the point."

"It's not the same." I sounded pretty complainy. But didn't I have good reason to complain? "Even Joon's snake has a special part."

She laughed. "I'm glad we'll be seeing Bagel on a screen and not slithering around the table. Do snakes even eat matzo?"

"Mom, it's not funny."

"It's kind of funny."

I closed my eyes and thought about what I really wanted to say. "I know the Seder is for all of us, but . . ."

"But you're growing up! Look at you. Braces. Bras. Body odor."

"MOM!"

"OK. OK. I think I get it. You're feeling overshadowed by the boys. You know, when I was about your age, Poppy's sister moved back here from London with her son."

"Cousin Alan?"

"Yeah. Aunt Maya and I had been the only two children at our Seders for years. But instead of being excited to see my cousin, I was jealous. Everyone fussed over this boy. The adults all thought Alan's British accent was *so* adorable and his manners were *so* polite."

"What did you do?" I asked. I'd never heard this story before.

"I told your nana I was feeling left out. She took me and Maya on a special girls-only trip to the pottery shop. We painted our Miriam's Cup together. It's been a special part of our Seder ever since."

The cup was goblet-shaped. On a pale blue background was a dancing woman with a rainbow-striped dress. Her mouth made an "O," exactly the way Ms. Krulik taught us to open our voices when we sang.

On the back of the cup were three words in English—*River, Sea, Well*—and one word in Hebrew, מִרְיָם. Miriam.

"I didn't know you *made* the cup," I said. "I thought it came from a store."

"Miriam's Cups were harder to find back then," Mom said. She stretched her arms and yawned. "Your poppy had never heard of them. He wanted to stick to the same old haggadah. We girls had to convince him that without Miriam, we wouldn't even have a Seder."

I knew what Mom meant. When Pharaoh made a decree to kill all of the Israelites' baby boys, Moses's mother, Yocheved, put him in a little ark and prayed that he'd float to safety. But it was Moses's big sister, Miriam, who climbed into the river and followed him. She hid in the reeds so she could watch over the baby. It was Miriam who made sure Moses was found by Pharaoh's kindhearted daughter. And Miriam told Pharaoh's daughter about the Hebrew woman,

Yocheved, who would make the perfect "nursemaid" for the baby. To me, Miriam was the ultimate big sister. Mom was right. Miriam played a big part in the Seder story.

"How did you get Poppy to change his mind?" I asked.

"Poppy will be here tomorrow," Mom said. "Why don't you ask him?"

※彡

The next day was Passover Eve. Our Seder would start at sundown. Nana and Poppy came over after lunch. Poppy got down on the floor and let Raffi and Jared climb all over him. Part of me wished I could get in there and wrestle, too, but Nana asked me to help her make the Seder Plate. By the time we'd finished, Poppy had sent the boys outside to play. He sat down at his spot with a cup of coffee and began marking the haggadah with a pencil.

"What are you doing?" I asked.

"Making preparations. A good leader must be prepared." Poppy held up two fingers. He was very proud of being an Eagle Scout. "First, I review the haggadah. And then," he pulled a folded printout from his pocket and spread it on the table.

On the top, it said in bold letters, "Moses and Pharaoh's Epic Battle."

Poppy said, "Your cousins asked me to narrate their skit."

I slumped. I shut my eyes so they wouldn't start leaking tears.

"What's wrong, bubbeleh?" Poppy asked.

"Sometimes I hate being the eldest *and* the only girl. I wish there was a special part in the Seder for me."

Poppy put an arm around my waist and gave me a half-squeeze. He said, "This haggadah belonged to my father. He made notes in the margins too, so even though he's gone, I know which phrases in the Seder used to make your mother laugh, which sections your great grandpa skipped, and who had favorite parts."

"The way Nana does the Ten Plagues?" I asked. She liked to say the Hebrew words in a super spooky voice. *Dam! Tzfardeiya! Kinim!* It always made the boys—and me—crack up.

Poppy turned to the Four Questions. On the side of the page was a list of names written in pencil. "In the time we have had this haggadah, my brother Dan read the Four Questions, then Maya, your mother, and Cousin Alan."

Underneath Alan's name was mine. *Hannah* it said in Poppy's neat handwriting.

"Cousin Alan must have been the youngest for a long time," I said.

Poppy nodded. "And now it's the boys' turn."

Under my name, he wrote, *Joon, Raffi, Tae, Jared.* None of the names on the list were crossed out. That made me feel proud, like I was helping pass the Seder tradition down to my brothers and cousins. The way my mother had once passed them to Cousin Alan.

"Poppy, there's a piece of paper stuck in there," I said. I'd never noticed it before.

Poppy turned to the back of the haggadah. A faded yellow note poked out of the pages. I recognized my mother's handwriting, only the letters were a little bigger and curlier than I was used to.

"Your mother wrote this note when she was your age."

Dear Father, I read. *We hereby request that you, as leader of our Seder, add Miriam's Cup to our Passover celebration to help us remember Miriam's part in the Passover story. Your daughters, Maya and Liz.*

"Why did they make it sound so fancy?" I asked.

"Who knows?" Poppy said. "I thought it was pretty funny. But your mother and aunt were very serious about it."

If Joon and Tae could add a skit to our Seder, and Mom and her sister brought Miriam's Cup into our family—even though it was a long time ago—maybe I could contribute something special to our Passover dinner, after all.

"Can I borrow the haggadah when you're finished, Poppy?" I asked.

"Sure thing. After I'm done here, I'll get to work on my world-famous matzo balls, and you may look at the haggadah to your heart's content."

Poppy makes the lightest, fluffiest matzo balls. Other people—Nana, my parents, Aunt Maya—have tried the recipe, but their matzo balls are lumpy and lopsided. Poppy has the special touch. When he finished looking over the hagga-dah and the boys' skit, Poppy went into the kitchen.

"Hannah, would you keep an eye on your brothers while we make the matzo balls?" my mom called.

"Sorry, Mom," I said. "There's something I need to do for myself first."

"They'll be fine for a few minutes, Liz," Poppy told my mom. He winked at me before heading into the kitchen, say-ing, "Where's my apron?"

I opened the haggadah. At the bottom of the yellow paper, kid-Mom had written one line about Miriam from the Book of Exodus. Miriam "took a timbrel in her hand, and all the women went out after her with timbrels and with dances." I had to look up the word "timbrel" online. It's an ancient hand drum, like a tambourine. Miriam was making music! It's one of the very first mentions of music in the entire Torah.

Miriam's name may not be mentioned in the traditional Haggadah (Moses's isn't either), but she's an important part of the story we tell on Passover. Not only was she there when Moses was adopted by Pharaoh's daughter, but as a grown woman, Miriam escaped Egypt with the rest of the Israelites, at the side of her brothers, Moses and Aaron. When the Red Sea came crashing down, Miriam wasn't afraid. I found the words that she sang: "Sing to the Eternal, for He has triumphed glori-ously; Horse and driver He has hurled into the sea."

This was a Miriam I could connect with. What did I do whenever I felt happy? I sang! I sang first thing in the morning (even though it annoyed my mother, who begged me to wait until she'd had her coffee). I sang to myself while I did my chores and even in the shower. Chorus was my favorite part of the school day because I didn't have to think about numbers, or facts, or analyzing poems. I could just open my mouth and let my feelings out.

Something else came up in my search: a video called "Miriam's Song."

I clicked. I listened. The song began with women's voices harmonizing, no words at first. I hummed along, trying to pick up the melody. The singers were a group of cantors, and the song was about Miriam, dancing with her timbrel. I got that strange feeling I always do when I hear a beautiful piece of music. My arms went chilly and prickly. My eyes got misty, like Nana's did when she heard me sing. I clicked repeat over and over, listening to the story of Miriam leading the women in celebration. The music and lyrics were by a famous Jewish songwriter named Debbie Friedman. How had I never heard of her before?

Could I be a leader, like Miriam? It was one thing to sing the Four Questions but another to introduce something new to my family's Passover celebration. Could I share my love of the Passover story with my family, the way Debbie Friedman had when she wrote this song? Maybe I'd grow up to be a songwriter like her someday.

※⁓⁓

I have to admit, the boys did a great job. They sang the Four Questions with so much enthusiasm, all the grown-ups cheered. Then, right before Nana's dramatic reading of the Ten Plagues, Joon and Tae put on costumes and performed their skit about Moses and Aaron confronting Pharaoh. Poppy's big voice made him the perfect narrator, and Uncle Jong-in looked hilarious in a striped-towel Pharaoh headdress. Bagel the ball python was more interested in snoozing than acting, but he made the scene feel realistic. Still, I was glad he was curled up on Joon's arm in California and not sitting next to me at the Seder table.

After the hunt for the afikomen (Jared got the prize: a Matchbox car). The adults drank their third glass of wine. Dad filled Elijah's cup and opened the front door. Poppy nodded at me. It was time.

I poured water into Miriam's cup, said a prayer, and took a sip.

I explained that the cup was a symbol of Miriam's Well, which the Israelites used for water while they wandered the desert. "Including the cup in our Seder reminds us that Miriam and other women were an important part of the Exodus story," I said. "And now, it's time for my big surprise."

"Another skit?" Poppy asked.

"Not exactly," I said. "The Bible says that when the Red Sea came crashing down on Pharaoh's army, Miriam led the women in celebration."

Mom smiled at me and nodded.

"I'm going to teach you a song about it."

I cued the music and began to sing about Miriam playing her hand drum and dancing in a circle of women. I'd thought about making this a girls-only part of the Seder, but it stinks to feel left out. Gathered around the table, my family also made a circle, everyone smiling as they joined in the song's chorus.

That's when I knew. I was going to perform "Miriam's Song" at my chorale audition. It was a song I felt with my whole heart. The melody would remind me of how the Seder was a living, changing tradition. Each year, my family gathered together, retelling an ancient story of fighting and snakes, floods and escapes, music and matzo. Remembering how I brought something new to our Seder would make me feel brave like Miriam, a girl who helped change history.

HALLEL

Nearly done now. This step is another long set of ancient prayers, mostly gratitude.

- At the end of Hallel, the fourth and final cup of wine or grape juice is drunk. This is not the only time the number four has come up in the Haggadah. It's a bit of a theme, this number. Can you recall when else it showed up? Why do you think this number is used multiple times in the Seder?

- There might be a lot of ways to celebrate the Seder night, but one thing many families have in common is reaching this step and being . . . tired. It's been a long night. And Hallel is not short. Some families might skip this step. Some families might abbreviate it. Some might speed-read through, quietly to themselves. Have you ever been impatient to finish something? Even something important to you? Something you enjoyed?

- Are you thankful for anything that happened long before you were born? Anything you might take for granted?

- Look around—right now, from where you're sitting—is there someone nearby you can thank for something? Will you? If not, who is the next person in your life you can thank?

DOUBLE HALLEL

WRITTEN AND ILLUSTRATED BY AMY IGNATOW

Our family Seders used to be longer. Of course, everything feels like it takes forever when you're a hungry kid who is expected to sit quietly in an uncomfortable dress, but in 1984 our family Seder actually took seventy-eight hours.

(This is not true. The Seder did not take seventy-eight hours, that's ridiculous, but I was only seven when this happened so a lot of the details are probably . . . slightly exaggerated. This is what we in the writing bizness call "being an unreliable narrator" or "taking poetic license" or "entertaining.")

That Seder would not have taken quite so long had it not been for The Plan, which my grandfather had concocted with stars in his eyes upon remembering that he had a reel-to-reel audio recorder in his basement.

Archie Ignatow, beloved grandfather and unskilled audio recording enthusiast

Hello beautiful!

With you I can record our ENTIRE SEDER.

Have you ever seen *Jurassic Park*? It's a movie where rogue scientists re-create dinosaurs who then run around killing people. In the movie, Jeff Goldblum, a fine Jewish actor playing a fine scientist, says of the project,

Your scientists were so preoccupied with whether or not they could that they didn't stop to think if they should.

The same could be said of my grandfather's plan to audio record the entire Seder. My own mother questioned it. "Are we ever going to listen to this?" she grumbled while sneaking small pieces of dry matzoh to me under the table to keep the recording free from my whining.

My grandfather had carefully placed his new microphone on the hanging lamp over the dining room table, and we were all instructed to speak loudly and clearly in the direction of that lamp. As a result, we conducted the entire Seder yelling toward the ceiling.

Baruch ata Adonai...

Ted! Face the lamp! Talk to the lamp!

No one was loud enough, which is wild because under normal circumstances we are an incredibly loud family.

But when faced with the task of recording the entire Seder for posterity, we were suddenly very meek.

I was the youngest kid there, but we were all suffering.

And then, at long last, we'd said all of the blessings and washed our hands and downed glasses of wine and grape juice and told the Passover story and asked the Four Questions and eaten the matzoh and the bitter herbs and finally it was time to eat our warm meal.

Nothing.

And so we did the entire Seder all over again, only this time we were on a mission: Finish this Seder as fast and as loud as possible so that we could finally eat the dinner my grandmother had been working on for days.

Some of us didn't make it.

But finally, after one hundred and twenty-four hours, we finished for the second time.

And that night, Archie Ignatow took his pencil to the leader's copy of the haggadah, cutting out the bits that he deemed unnecessary, figuring that twice all the way through was enough for at least the next couple of decades.

Over the years, we've inadvertently created new traditions to our Seder—not a year goes by when we don't mention the time Grandpa tried to record the whole thing. (We also always bring up the time he misread the plague of gnats as a plague of "goats" and then insisted that he was right.)

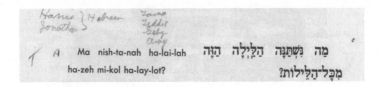

My grandfather passed away in 1992, and my Uncle Richard continued to use his abridged haggadah to lead our Seders. Then a few years ago, I was given the family haggadah to continue the tradition.

It's been nearly forty years since that long, long night, and my family has never again done the full, unedited Seder. But talking about the time we did has become the part of the Seder that we enjoy the most.*

---

* This is untrue, my Aunt Paula's matzoh ball soup is the part of the Seder that we enjoy the most.

NIRTZAH

Nirtzah, the final step. An ending, sort of. Just a few lines: wishes for the future and a declaration that the Seder is over . . . followed by pages and pages of extra songs. Maybe the songs are part of Nirtzah, maybe not. Maybe a family will sing all of them, some, or none at all. But the songs are *there*, in case we're not quite ready to leave. Not just yet.

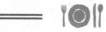

- *Have you ever reached the end of something and didn't want to go?*

- *Have you ever seen a movie that ended with the credits rolling, while a song played in the background? Is that song part of the movie? Why or why not?*

- *One of the more famous songs at the end of the Seder is called "Chad Gadya," or "One Little Goat." It's a bit like "There Was an Old Woman Who Swallowed a Fly," only with a cat and a dog and the Angel of Death. On the surface, the song has nothing to do with Passover, and yet it feels like it does. Do you have a favorite song that, on the surface, has nothing to do with you, and yet it feels like it does?*

- *This time next year, where do you hope to be? Who do you hope to be?*

JUST JAYA

VEERA HIRANANDANI

Jaya's legs bounced up and down. She couldn't wait to get out of the car after the four-hour ride to the ferry. She watched out the window as they drove right onto the bottom of the enormous boat. After they parked, they could roam around the upper deck. The moment her father turned off the ignition, she sprang into the parking lot and up the stairs leading to freedom.

"Be careful," both her parents called out to her as she started up the stairwell. Jaya slowed down a little until she was out of sight and then ran the rest of the way. She pushed open the heavy metal door leading to the windy deck and went right up to the railing, gazing out at the expanse of water as the ferry boat churned along. The fresh salty air filled her lungs as she took deep breaths, just like Grammy Malka always told her to do when she stood before the ocean. She watched the seagulls swoop and dive along with the current of the boat, and after a little while, the island came into view.

"There it is!" she called to her parents, who were sitting on a bench nearby. They looked out and smiled.

"Grammy can't wait to see you. Ava and Orly are already there," her father said. Jaya smiled back, but the fact that her cousins, Ava and Orly, had arrived earlier stiffened her jaw. As the boat got closer, she wished she could spy on them through Grammy Malka's windows and know what exactly they were doing before she got there, but the house wasn't that near the shore.

As an only child, she loved to plop herself in the middle of Ava and Orly's warm, buzzing, sometimes competitive sister energy. Often she imagined they were all sisters, and at eleven, she fit right in the middle, age-wise. This fall though, Ava was having her bat mitzvah, and it was all she talked about with Grammy. This made Jaya wonder if Grammy liked Ava and Orly better than she liked her.

They visited Grammy Malka on Martha's Vineyard many times throughout the spring and summer. She lived alone. Jaya's grandfather died from cancer when Jaya was only three, and she hardly remembered him. Grammy had an apartment in Boston as well, but it was much more fun to visit the small, gray-shingled house on the island, and Passover was when Grammy "opened" it up for the season.

It was the kind of house where no one had to worry if they got sand on the scuffed wooden floors or sat on the faded couch in a wet bathing suit. It was the place where her whole family seemed relaxed and happy. Well, they were in the summer, but not on Passover—at least not Jaya.

She couldn't tell anyone this, though. She knew Ava and Orly didn't feel the same. They always wore fancy dresses for the Seder and helped make most of the food. Jaya didn't go to Hebrew school like Ava and Orly. She wasn't planning on having a bat mitzvah, either. Ava and Orly thought this meant she was Hindu like her mother, not Jewish like her father. But Jaya didn't feel more one religion than the other. She was just Jaya.

When the ferry docked in Oak Bluffs, they hurried back down to their car, drove off the boat, through the busy town, and onto a quieter road where they passed farms, meadows, long stone walls, and rows of blooming daffodils. The air smelled like wet dirt, fresh rain, and everything new. They reached the bumpy dirt road that led to the little house at the end. Her grandmother had painted the front door a bright yellow that reminded Jaya of the flowers she had seen on the way.

They parked, got their bags, and walked right in. Ava and Orly sat in the living room playing hearts with Grammy around the coffee table. Jaya stood behind her parents as everyone got up and started hugging. She stayed behind, not quite ready.

Grammy came over in her multicolored caftan and her curly gray hair tumbling down her back. Jaya's father told her once that Grammy used to sing and play guitar in a rock band before she became a music teacher at the nursery school in her synagogue.

Grammy put her hands on Jaya's shoulders.

"Look at you," she said. "In only six months, you're a different person!"

Jaya smiled and felt the heat grow in her cheeks. That's what Grammy usually said when she first saw her, and Jaya wondered why she always looked like a different person to Grammy. Was she not looking closely enough? Suddenly Ava grabbed her hand.

"Let me show you the new beds!"

"Yeah!" Orly said and started up the stairs.

Jaya grabbed her duffle bag and let Ava pull her to the girls' room, as they called it. There was a new white bunk bed on one side and the old single bed on the other. A bunch of daffodils sat in a vase on the dresser, though not all the blooms had opened yet. Flowy white curtains moved to the rhythm of the oscillating fan. Jaya wished it was summer already, wished that they could skip right to that part.

"Grammy said I get the top since I'm the oldest," Ava said. "But don't worry, you get your own bed."

Jaya nodded.

"I wanted the bottom bunk anyway. It has a shelf for my stuffies," Orly called out. She had more stuffed animals than anyone Jaya knew and traveled with no fewer than ten.

"What are you going to wear?" Ava asked.

"When?" Jaya replied.

"Tonight of course! For the Seder." Before Jaya could answer, Ava ran over to show Jaya her new sundress hanging in the closet. It was pale green with tiny pink flowers.

"Pretty," Jaya said.

"Show me yours," Ava said, but Jaya was looking at her bed, which suddenly seemed lonely on the other side of the room. She liked it better when there were three beds, one against each wall. There was hardly space to walk, but it felt cozier that way, like they were all the same.

"I'm wearing this," she said, looking down at her blue T-shirt dress. It kept her comfortable during the long Seder.

"Oh," Ava said. "Didn't you wear that last year?"

"Maybe," said Jaya, not remembering.

"Orly is wearing a dress from last year, too. My mom only gets us new dresses when we grow out of the old ones, no matter how much we beg her."

"Yeah," Jaya said. "Me too." But she didn't beg her mom for dresses. She was more likely to beg for polymer clay or a new paint set.

"Later I'll show you pictures of my bat mitzvah dress. Want to go back down?"

"OK," Jaya said, and she followed her cousins down the stairs.

Before Jaya knew it, the Seder started, led by Grammy. Jaya once told this to Rebecca, her only close Jewish friend at school. Rebecca was surprised. "I didn't know women led Seders. I thought only the men did."

Jaya had shrugged. Grammy's Seders were all she knew. Grammy used Jaya's grandfather's haggadah. Before he died, he had taken parts from different haggadahs he liked, written some of his own interpretations, and typed it up. Her father said using the haggadah was a way that Grammy kept him alive in her mind. Jaya thought that was nice, but she didn't like that it was much longer than the old Maxwell House Haggadahs they also put out but never used.

The candles were lit and they began. Her parents sat on one end with her Aunt Nancy and Uncle Josh. She sat on the other with Ava and Orly, and Grammy sat at the head with a pillow under her arm. Jaya followed along as best she could, Grammy beaming at both Ava and Orly as they proudly recited many of the sections in Hebrew. Jaya wondered if she'd ever seen Grammy look at her that way. She managed to get through most of the parts without feeling too bored. She even ate the little bowl full of boiled potato, egg, and a sprig of parsley in salt water that was supposed to remind her of tears. Jaya had to admit that eating a hard-boiled egg swimming in cloudy salt water did make her want to cry.

Jaya's stomach started grumbling again when they got to the part where they made little sandwiches out of the charoset, Jaya's favorite Passover food. She and her mother made the charoset together every year, blending the apples, walnuts, and sweet wine in a food processor. Her mother even put in a sprinkle of ground cardamom as her special touch, since many Indian sweets had cardamom in them.

They finally got to the main meal. This was when Jaya could relax and have seconds of Grammy's delicious matzo ball soup.

"So," Grammy said as they ate, "Jaya, how's the flute?"

Jaya looked at her mother and back at Grammy. "Oh, I don't play the flute."

Grammy squinted.

"I'm the one who plays, Grammy," said Ava.

"That's right!" Grammy said.

"She played a solo in her last recital," Aunt Nancy said, smiling at Ava. "And she's going to play something for the bat mitzvah."

"I'm glad my musical genes have been passed on," Grammy said. "Jaya, remind me, what activities do you do these days?"

Jaya wondered how Grammy could get mixed up like that. Jaya was terrible at playing instruments. She had tried the drums for a little while, but her parents seemed relieved when she stopped. She preferred art.

"I'm taking pottery and watercolor painting," she answered.

"Oh lovely," Grammy replied, then started talking to Ava about what flute piece she was playing for her bat mitzvah.

After a while, Jaya was relieved they had moved on from the bat mitzvah, but the conversation kept returning to Ava.

Grammy asked Ava what classes she was taking in seventh grade. Grammy also asked about her family's recent trip to France and how Ava's French lessons were going. Orly would jump into the conversation randomly to add a bit of competition to it all. Orly already knew fifteen French words. Orly could play all the same songs that Ava did on flute. As Jaya watched, she felt like she was growing smaller and smaller and might disappear into her chair.

About an hour later, her belly full of potato kugel, brisket, and her favorite chocolate macaroons, she knew the Seder still wasn't finished. They all helped take their plates into the kitchen and returned to the table. When Grammy opened up the haggadah again, Jaya wanted to run upstairs and dive into her bed. Wasn't everyone tired? Hadn't they done enough? She looked at her grandmother, who didn't look tired at all. She looked *too* energetic, her eyes darting around, her voice loud and high-pitched.

Her father poured more wine and grape juice for them, to fill the fourth cup as the haggadah directed. Her father had once told her they didn't really drink all four cups of wine, but only poured a little in their glass every time the haggadah said to drink another cup. Then they poured a cup for the prophet Elijah, who was supposed to come and visit, and set it in the middle of the table. Ava and Orly raced to open the door and then ran back to the table to see if the level of the wine would magically go down.

"It's going down. It is, look!" Orly yelled.

It looked the same to Jaya, but she didn't want to ruin Orly's excitement.

They went through the last steps, time moving more slowly in Jaya's eyes, which were becoming heavier and heavier. Finally, they came to the last part, which Grammy called Nirtzah.

"Oh, Daniel," Grammy said to Jaya's father, "remember how you used to sing 'One Only Kid' with Daddy in Hebrew? Will you sing it with Jaya? Jaya, go stand by Dad." She pointed to the page in the haggadah.

"Ma, we've all had a long day," her father said, probably noticing the heaviness in Jaya's eyes. "Why don't we just sing it all together?"

"That sounds like a plan," her mother said, stretching her arms up into the air and winking at Jaya.

Grammy's face fell. "Well, if you don't want to, I'll sing it with Jaya. Come, sweetheart. You've been so quiet. Stand by me," she said.

Jaya held on to the edge of her chair. Suddenly everyone was looking at her.

Orly must have noticed Jaya's hesitation. "I can do it, Grammy. I'm the youngest, so I'm supposed to," she said, getting up. Jaya relaxed, this time happy for her cousin to take over.

"At least let Jaya start it," Grammy said to Orly and held her arm out to Jaya. "I don't want her to feel left out. Here.

Follow this," she said and handed her the other haggadah, where the Hebrew was spelled out in English.

Jaya glanced at her father, a pleading look in her eye. He only motioned his chin in Grammy Malka's direction. Her mother just shrugged and gave her a weak smile, so she got up and walked slowly over to Grammy. Grammy put her arm around Jaya's waist and pulled her close, too close. Then Grammy pointed to the song and started. Jaya tried to keep up, but when Ava and Orly eventually joined in on the next verses, following along, clear and loud, Jaya didn't even want to try anymore. She saw her mother, who didn't know Hebrew either, but somehow was moving her lips anyway. She saw her father, his head down, murmuring into the pages.

She remembered as a younger child liking the song in English, thinking it was fun as they all tried to keep up with the verses that got longer and faster as the song went on. But she couldn't understand the Hebrew verses that just grew louder. Grammy held on to her around the waist. Her face felt hot and she wanted it all to stop, but what could she say? Then tears started to bloom, and she didn't want anyone to see them fall. She broke away from Grammy and ran upstairs, ignoring the gasps and then Grammy calling her.

When she got to her room, she flung herself onto the bed, got under the quilt, and let herself cry a little. After a few minutes, she heard slow grown-up footsteps coming up the stairs, and she pulled the quilt over her head. She felt someone sit down. Then she heard Grammy say her name. Jaya didn't answer.

"I'm sorry, Jaya," Grammy said. "Please, can I see your face?" Jaya shook her head under the covers.

"I didn't mean to make you uncomfortable."

Jaya pulled down the covers a little bit, just showing her eyes. "Maybe I shouldn't come to Passover anymore," she said in a whisper.

Grammy opened her mouth slightly. "Why would you say that?" she asked.

"Because I'm not really Jewish," she said, now staring hard at Grammy. She knew Grammy would tell her that she was, that even if she didn't practice at home, she was part of a Jewish family. She would tell her that Jaya was just as welcome as anyone and that she was her granddaughter and that she loved her. Grammy did say all of those things and Jaya nodded along. It wasn't the first time Grammy noticed Jaya's discomfort. It wasn't the first time Grammy had reminded her of these things.

"But I know you know all that," Grammy said. "Passover is a hard holiday for me, too."

"It *is*?" Jaya said, now pulling the covers farther down her face.

"I feel so much pressure. It takes a lot out of me."

"It does?" Jaya said and took off the covers, sitting up.

"It was so important to your grandfather. That's why he wrote his own haggadah before he died. I feel like if I don't do it the way he wanted, I'm not honoring his memory." Grammy looked down at her lap. "I'm not even that religious. I'm just an old ex-hippy," she said and laughed. "I didn't mean to push the Hebrew on you. I just wanted you to feel a part of things."

Jaya took this all in. "I'm different than Ava and Orly."

"We're all different," Grammy said.

"I'm not Jewish in the way they are. In the way that you are."

"You know you don't have to be," Grammy said.

Jaya took a deep breath and said what she had wanted to say for a long time. "But Passover makes me feel like I do."

They sat quietly for a minute.

"Isn't Passover about freedom?" Jaya then asked, slowly. "About the Jews freeing themselves from slavery in Egypt?"

"Yes," Grammy said and took off her glasses. She started cleaning them with part of her dress. She turned to Jaya.

"So shouldn't everyone feel free to be themselves at the Seder? You should celebrate Passover the way you want to. And I should, too. Grandpa wouldn't want you to be so stressed."

Grammy put her glasses back on and looked at Jaya, really looked at her.

"He wouldn't want you to be, either. You're so smart, Jaya. You grow wiser every year. It takes my breath away," Grammy said.

"You think that?" She wondered if this was why her grandmother always said she looked like a different person.

Grammy nodded. "You've already figured out the true meaning of Passover and as you said, you're not even 'really' Jewish."

"OK," Jaya said. "I guess I am a little."

"It's up to you to decide how Jewish you are."

"Maybe we could sing more of the songs in English next year," Jaya said in a small voice.

Grammy reached over and squeezed Jaya's hand. "I think that could be arranged," she said.

Then Grammy's eyes landed on the vase of daffodils.

"How beautiful!" she exclaimed. Jaya turned and looked at them. The blossoms had all opened. "Let's bring them down and put them on the table. They'll look so nice in the morning. For breakfast, I'm making matzo brei the way you like it, with cinnamon and sugar."

Jaya smiled. She did like Grammy's matzo brei. She got out of bed and picked up the vase, letting the silky petals tickle her chin. She stood up a little straighter and decided that for next Passover she wouldn't be afraid to speak up and say what she was comfortable doing. She didn't have to feel bad for not knowing the Hebrew. She could celebrate in her way, not just in the way that she thought she was supposed to. She hoped Grammy would do the same.

She followed Grammy down the stairs, holding the vase, already thinking about being back here in the summer, the freedom of it so close she could almost touch it.

RECIPES

WE STILL DON'T WANT TO LEAVE.

Like the traditional Haggadah, we wanted to include something else to keep you here with us, just a little longer. So we've collected what we hope is as fun as a song about one little goat: A few recipes, created especially for this anthology. We're so excited to share them with you, and for you to share them with your family and friends.

Don't forget to always be safe in the kitchen and work with a grown-up when needed.

KUAJADO DE ESPINAKA KON KESO

BY SUSAN BAROCAS

Serves 4 to 6

This Sephardic dish of vegetables, eggs, and cheese—cooked together in a casserole—goes by many names, most often "kuajado" in Ladino (also spelled "cuajado" and "quajado"). For hundreds of years, these dishes were so important to the Jews of Spain that kuajado was mentioned many times during Inquisition trials as proof of being Jewish. The vegetables used most often were eggplant, leeks, zucchini, and greens such as chard and spinach. Even today, kuajados are still beloved by Sephardim whose ancestors, when expelled from Spain beginning in 1492, found safe haven in the lands of the Ottoman Empire. Even if you don't think you like spinach, try this dish; it just might change your mind.

INGREDIENTS

2 tablespoons olive oil

8 large eggs

15 ounces (about 12 cups loosely packed) fresh baby
  spinach, washed

½ cup crumbled feta cheese

1 cup grated Parmesan

1 tablespoon matzah meal

½ teaspoon salt or to taste

¼ teaspoon ground black pepper to taste

WHAT TO DO

Preheat oven to 375°F. Put the olive oil in a 9-inch by 9-inch baking pan, then swirl the oil around slowly to cover the entire bottom and some of the sides of the pan. Set aside.

In a large mixing bowl, use a fork or whisk to beat the eggs until well blended.

Working in handfuls, cut or tear the spinach, including the stems, into very small pieces, like skinny ribbons. Put the spinach in the bowl with the beaten eggs. Taste the feta to see how salty it is, then add the feta, Parmesan, matzah meal, salt (use less or none if your feta is especially salty), and pepper to the spinach and eggs. Use a big spoon to mix everything very thoroughly, making sure to scoop up and include all the eggs at the bottom of the bowl.

Put the pan with the oil in the oven—remember, the oven is already hot!—for about 3 to 4 minutes. Carefully take it out of the oven and set it on a heatproof surface or the stovetop.

Working quickly (and carefully), put all of the mixture into the pan. It should sizzle, which will help create a nice crust on the bottom. Use the back of a large spoon to spread out the mixture evenly, making sure to fill the corners!

Bake, uncovered, for about 35 to 40 minutes until the center is firm to the touch and the edges are golden brown. Let cool for about 15 minutes before cutting. Serve warm or at room temperature. Refrigerate leftovers for 5 days or freeze, then defrost and reheat, uncovered, 10 to 12 minutes in a 350°F oven.

Chef, cooking instructor, and writer **Susan Barocas** *is passionate about healthy, no-waste cooking and Jewish food, especially Sephardic history, culture, and cuisines. She has cooked and taught all over the world and was guest chef for three seders in the Obama White House. Susan is cofounder/ codirector of the new project Savor: A Sephardic Music & Food Experience (savorexperience.com). Follow Susan on Instagram and Facebook using her name.*

CAPRESE MATZO PIZZA

BY EITAN BERNATH

Makes 4 matzos

Caprese Matzo Pizza takes everything you love about matzo pizza and caprese salad, and makes it both quicker to make and easier to eat! The pesto comes together in the time it takes the oven to preheat, so you can have these delicious matzo pizzas ready in 20 minutes flat. The drizzle of balsamic glaze at the end takes them to the next level—you'll believe me once you try it!

INGREDIENTS

For the Pesto

2 cups packed fresh basil leaves

1 garlic clove

¼ cup grated Parmesan cheese

Juice of ½ lemon

½ cup extra-virgin olive oil

Salt and pepper, to taste

For the Pizza

4 sheets matzo

1 cup tomato sauce

One 8-ounce ball fresh mozzarella, sliced

2 ripe roma tomatoes, sliced
Salt and pepper, to taste
Balsamic glaze, for drizzling

WHAT TO DO

First, make the pesto. Add the basil, garlic, Parmesan, and lemon juice to a food processor or blender and blend until very finely chopped. Stream in the olive oil with the machine running on low until a thick sauce forms. Taste the pesto and add salt and pepper as needed. Transfer to a resealable container and refrigerate until ready to use.

Next, make the pizza. Preheat the oven to 425°F and line a sheet pan with parchment paper.

Place the matzo on a clean surface with all toppings nearby. Spread ¼ cup of the tomato sauce onto each matzo, leaving a ½ inch crust on the edges. Divide the cheese evenly among them, followed by the tomatoes. Season the tomatoes with salt and pepper, if desired.

Place the matzo pizzas onto the prepared sheet pan and bake for 10 minutes, or until the cheese is bubbling and beginning to brown.

Place the pan on a cooling rack and allow the pizzas to cool for 5 minutes before drizzling with the pesto. Drizzle with balsamic glaze, if desired. Serve immediately.

Eitan Bernath *is an award-winning chef, author, TV personality, entertainer, and social justice activist. With over eight million followers and three billion annual video views, he is the chief executive officer of Eitan Productions, the Principal Culinary Contributor for the Daytime Emmy® award-winning* Drew Barrymore Show *on CBS, and is a contributor to the* Washington Post, Food & Wine, Saveur, *and* Delish. *His work has been recognized by publications including the* New York Times, Vanity Fair, Rolling Stone, New York Magazine, *and* People.

SEPHARDIC COCO

BY HÉLÈNE JAWHARA PIÑER

Makes 15 pieces

This special recipe—which requires supervision of adults (as all do, of course)—makes 15 delicious Sephardic treats called "coco." You might know versions of them as macaroons—and now you and your family can make some yourselves! Enjoy!

INGREDIENTS

6 oz sugar
3.5 oz egg whites
4.5 oz coconut powder
2 tablespoons applesauce
1 tablespoon orange marmalade

WHAT TO DO

Preheat the oven to 350°F and boil 5 cups of water in a pan. Meanwhile, combine the sugar and egg whites in a heatproof bowl (or a pot or the top section of a double-boiler). Stir well!

Very carefully—and remember, with grown-ups only!—set the bowl over the pan of boiling water, making sure the bottom of the bowl does not touch the water. While one person holds the bowl and heats the egg white–sugar mixture, their partner should be stirring constantly for 3 to 5 minutes, until the sugar dissolves and the mixture becomes smooth.

Remove the bowl from the heat and add the coconut powder, applesauce, and orange marmalade. Mix until the batter is thoroughly combined.

Line a baking sheet with parchment paper. Using a spoon, drop 15 scoops of the batter onto the parchment paper, leaving about 1 inch of space between them. Bake for 13 minutes. Let the macaroons cool for about 10 minutes before eating. You can store them in a box and keep for 2 days. If you store the box in the fridge, you can keep for at least 4 days, if you have any left by then!

Hélène Jawhara Piñer is a PhD in Medieval History and the History of Food and was awarded the Broome & Allen Fellowship from the American Sephardi Federation in 2018. In 2021, she spearheaded the culinary live shows Sephardic Culinary History, *promoted by the American Sephardi Federation & The Center of Jewish History. She is the author of* Sephardi: Cooking the History, Recipes of the Jews of Spain and the Diaspora from the 13th Century to Today, *and* Jews, Food and Spain: The Oldest Medieval Spanish Cookbook and the Sephardic Culinary Heritage.

MILK CHOCOLATE ALMOND MATZA TOFFEE

BY ADEENA SUSSMAN

Serves 8 to 10

This version of the classic Passover treat uses milk chocolate and almonds, but the varieties are endless. I actually didn't grow up eating this delicacy, but in my adult life, it has become a staple that is requested on the eight days of Passover and beyond. It's flexible—use the chocolate and nuts of your choice (I love mine extra toasty and salty). Feel free to adjust these elements to your liking. Pack up batches for house gifts, and keep the toffee in the fridge for a cool bite.

INGREDIENTS

5 or 6 square matzas, preferably thin "tea" matzas and salted

2 sticks (1 cup) unsalted butter, coconut oil, or margarine

1 cup packed light brown sugar

Three 3.5-ounce milk chocolate bars (about 2 cups finely chopped)

1½ teaspoons Maldon sea salt flakes (I prefer Maldon, but any will do)

1½ cups roasted salted almonds, chopped

WHAT TO DO

Preheat the oven to 350°F.

Line the bottom and sides of a large (12-inch by 17-inch) baking sheet with aluminum foil. Arrange the matzas on the sheet. (A grown-up can use a serrated knife to gently saw off parts of each matza so they fit in a single layer, like a jigsaw puzzle! If you don't feel like being a geek like me, just snap the matzas and be kind to yourself about the inevitably shattered matzas.)

In a 3-quart saucepan over medium-low heat, bring the butter and brown sugar to a boil, stirring constantly and lowering the flame if needed to keep the boiling in control. Continue stirring until a smooth caramel forms, about 3 minutes. Quickly pour the bubbling caramel over the matza, smooth it out a little with a spatula (an offset spatula, if you've got one), and bake until browned and the edges burn slightly, 17 to 18 minutes (if you like your matza less on-the-edge-of-burnt, bake for 15 minutes).

Remove from the oven, sprinkle the chocolate on top, and return to the oven for 30 seconds to help it melt. Remove the pan from the oven and let the chocolate melt a little more, 1 to 2 minutes. Using that spatula again, spread the chocolate evenly all over, cool for 1 minute, sprinkle the surface of the chocolate with the salt, then sprinkle with the almonds. Chill, uncovered, until solid, 40 to 45 minutes, then have fun breaking it apart with your hands! (Or cut it into even slices with the serrated knife.) Store the toffee in the fridge in an airtight container for up to 2 weeks.

Adeena Sussman *is the author of the cookbook* Shabbat: Recipes and Rituals from My Table to Yours. *It is the followup to* Sababa, *which was named a Best Fall 2019 cookbook by the* New York Times, Bon Appetit, *and* Food & Wine. *The coauthor of 15 cookbooks, Adeena's three most recent collaborations, including* Cravings *and* Cravings: Hungry for More *with Chrissy Teigen, were* New York Times *bestsellers. A lifelong visitor to Israel who has been writing about that country's food culture for almost twenty years, Adeena lives, cooks, and writes in Tel Aviv, where she lives in the shadow of that city's Carmel Market with her husband, Jay Shofet. You can follow her on Instagram* @adeenasussman.

SUPER EASY PASSOVER COOKIES

BY MOLLY YEH

Makes 12

These cookies are so easy to make! One-bowl, three-minute easy. Delicious and satisfying, they get a crisp, crunchy shell but stay so amazingly chewy inside. Happy Passover!

INGREDIENTS

1 cup almond flour
1 cup hazelnut flour, or 1 more cup almond flour
½ cup lightly packed light brown sugar
½ cup granulated sugar
¾ teaspoon kosher salt
1 large egg
1 tablespoon vanilla extract
½ teaspoon almond extract
Coarse sanding sugar or turbinado sugar

WHAT TO DO

Preheat the oven to 350°F. In a large bowl, combine the almond flour, hazelnut flour, brown sugar, granulated sugar, and salt. Add the egg, vanilla, and almond extract (or experiment with other extracts, like orange or lemon), and stir to combine.

The whole mixture might seem dry at first, but don't give up! Keep on stirring (maybe ask a friend for help if your arm gets tired!) and it will come together. When it does, roll the dough into balls that are slightly bigger than golf balls. (You can also mix in 3 oz of coconut, chocolate chips, butterscotch or white chocolate chips! Mix and match! Come up with your own combinations!) Then roll the balls in sanding sugar (or maybe rainbow sprinkles!). Flatten them a little and then place them on a parchment paper–lined baking sheet, about 1 inch apart.

Bake for around 15 minutes, until lightly browned on the bottom. Let them cool slightly (don't burn your tongue!) and enjoy! They will be super gooey when they come out of the oven but they will get chewy as they cool.

Molly Yeh is the Emmy- and James Beard Award–nominated star of Food Network's series Girl Meets Farm, *which celebrates the very best of Molly's food, with recipes inspired by her Jewish and Chinese heritage and a taste of the Midwest. Yeh is also the author of the* New York Times *bestselling* Home Is Where the Eggs Are: Farmhouse Food for the People You Love *and* Molly on the Range: Recipes and Stories from an Unlikely Life on a Farm. *She lives on a sugar beet farm on the North Dakota–Minnesota border with her fifth-generation farmer husband, Nick, and their two daughters.*

ACKNOWLEDGMENTS

Who knows one? We know one. One is our editor, Erica Finkel, who understood this project from the start and helped shape it—every story, every page—into the best version of itself. We are so very grateful.

Who knows two? We know two. Two are . . . our fellow coeditors. Josh and Naomi, to Chris. Chris and Naomi, to Josh. Josh and Chris, to Naomi. We met the year before our debut novels came out, trekking up the snow-covered mountains to Highlights (Chris literally—and maybe also metaphorically?—pushing the stalled car up the hill), and we instantly knew that we were family. Fitting because, for all of us, "Found Families" have been as important as the ones we were born with. And we are honored to have brought together another family of sorts in this collection of stories. The collaboration has been a privilege and a joy.

Who knows three? We know three. Three are our agents, without whom this book wouldn't exist: Rena Rossner, Elana Roth Parker, and Liza Fleissig. Thanks for this project, and all the others.

Who knows four? We know four. Four is a theme on Passover, which we mentioned earlier. Four cups. The Four Questions. Four sons/children. (There's more, too: Four ancient names for the holiday. Four traditional stages of the Exodus.) And we've tried to build on the number: Four of our own questions before each story. Four(ish) recipes in the back. What we're trying to say is that themes, motifs—they've existed for us as long as we can remember. We're storytellers, from a tradition of storytelling. It is a privilege to be part of this chain.

Who knows five? We know five. Five are our fellow JPST kindred spirits: Jessica Kramer, Rajani LaRocca, Cory Leonardo, Gillian McDunn, and Nicole Pantaleakos. We never would have found each other—and the idea for this book—without the space this group of extraordinary writer-friends provides. Next up: The Codfather?

Who knows six? Josh knows six: I'm impossibly grateful to everyone who's helped bring this book to life. And, for me, that includes everyone who's brought other books to life as well. Nahum M. Sarna's *Exploring Exodus*, which I've never stopped reading. Baruch M. Bokser's *The Origins of the Seder*, which transformed how I think about this holiday (and everything else). Vanessa L. Ochs' *The Passover Haggadah: A Biography*, one of the best books about a book about a story from another book I've ever read. And, of course, the Haggadah itself: the little Elie Wiesel volume, never not under my skin; the New American Haggadah, such a lovely reflection of how the old can be new; and my tattered "Chief Rabbi's Haggadah" by Jonathan Sacks. Thank you for enriching my life all these years. Hoping that, in some small way, we're paying it forward.

Who knows seven? We know seven. Seven are (AT LEAST) all the ways one could spell the word "matzah" in English. (Matza? Matzoh? Matzo? Matso? Matsoh? Etc. etc. etc.) Although some spelling and capitalization has been standardized across the stories, we've left this word (and some others, too) deliberately alone, spelled however the underlying writer chose to spell it. One of the things we are most proud of in this collection is its *lack* of uniformity. We know: The book does not capture the full spectrum of the Jewish American experience. We know, Rabbi Tarfon, the work is unfinished. Guess we're all just going to have to keep writing, keep supporting each other, until everyone's story is told.

Who knows eight? Naomi knows eight: Passover has always been my favorite holiday because it meant family. The guests have changed over the years (from my first nuclear family to my second; from college professors to a new daughter-in-law), but Passover still means family to me—including my "family" of first readers: Malayna Evans, Rosa Hsiung, Penny March, Laura Shovan, Liz Sues, and especially my son, Jesse Milliner. Since family is so important to me, my young heroine in "Chocolate Tears"—Rachel—is named after my mother, Freeda Rachel Wender. And Rachel's grandmother is named after my own, Clara Keller. I was not lucky enough to meet her but have always felt a special connection with her. I like to think both she and my mom would love this anthology as much as I do.

Who knows nine? Chris knows nine: Thank you to my Aunt Edie and Uncle Paul, my cousins, my grandparents, Sam and Mae Rosensweig, and of course, Aunt Cookie. Thank you to all the other ancestors who kept this tradition alive so it could find its way to us and beyond. And thank you to my mom and dad, Hyacinthe and Ed, who always made sure I remembered the sacred.

Who knows ten? We know ten. Ten are just some of the other folks who have had a hand in making this book a reality. With Abrams: Emily Daluga (associate editor); Maggie Lehrman (editorial director); Maggie Moore (production manager); Marie Oishi (managing editor); Micah Fleming (design manager); and Melissa Greenberg (designer). Others, too, some of whom (as of this writing, at least) are not yet named: publicity and marketing team; copyeditor, Penelope Cray; proofreader, Margo Winton Parodi. And of course our illustrator: Shannon Hochman. Thank you thank you thank you.

Who knows eleven? We know eleven. Eleven are the incomparable story contributors to this anthology: Mari Lowe, R.M. Romero, Laurel Snyder, Adam Gidwitz, Sofiya Pasternack, Ruth Behar, Sarah Kapit, A. J. Sass, Laura Shovan, Amy Ignatow, and Veera Hiranandani. Your unique voices; your incredible writing talent—you brought to this project everything we'd hoped for. We don't have the words to express our appreciation. But from here on out, every Passover, we'll be raising a cup of wine (or four) to each of you. L'Chaim.

Who knows twelve? We know twelve. Twelve are the members of our families. Immediate families, anyway. Ella, Sasha, Samaria, and Caylao Baron. Tali, Serena, Henry, and Micah Levy. Lee, Jeremy, Jesse, and Jake Milliner. All of you are always enough.

ABOUT THE AUTHORS

Mari Lowe (she/her) loves making cat noises at Chad Gadya (if she isn't asleep on the couch), refuses to eat any dessert containing potato starch, and would happily hold a dozen Seders a year. As a middle school teacher at an Orthodox Jewish school and the daughter of a rabbi, she loves sharing glimpses into her community with her books. Her debut novel, *Aviva vs. the Dybbuk*, won the 2023 Sydney Taylor Book Award. She lives in New York with her family, menagerie of pets, and robotic vacuum.

———

R.M. Romero (she/they) is the author of fairy tales for children and adults. Her work includes international bestseller and Sydney Taylor Notable Book *The Dollmaker of Kraków*, Jewish National Book Award Finalist and Sydney Taylor Notable Book *The Ghosts of Rose Hill*, and *A Warning About Swans*, as well as the forthcoming *Death's Country* and *Tale of the Flying Forest*. She lives in Miami Beach with her feline companion Henry VIII and spends her summers maintaining Jewish cemeteries in Poland. Ms. Romero's favorite part of the Seder is opening the door for Elijah. (She has a fondness for ghosts.)

Naomi Milliner (she/her) is the author of *Super Jake & the King of Chaos* and the forthcoming *The Trouble with Secrets*. She created the Author Book Club for her SCBWI chapter and has served on The Women's National Book Association's Great Group Reads committee since 2009. Naomi enjoys mentoring children and adults, visiting schools (virtually or in-person), and reading everything she can get her hands on. She lives in Maryland with her family, a very fuzzy cat . . . and fifteen different haggadahs. One of the most delicious Seders she ever attended was a chocolate Seder.

Joshua S. Levy (he/him) is the author of several middle grade novels, including *Seventh Grade vs. the Galaxy* (and its sequels) and *The Jake Show*. Born and raised in Florida, Josh lives with his family in New Jersey, where he spent a little while teaching middle school and now practices as a lawyer. Josh treats himself to a new haggadah every year, which his family is definitely always super excited to hear all about throughout the Seder, right? (Right?!)

Laurel Snyder (she/her) is the author of many books for young readers, including *The Witch of Woodland*, a novel about a Jewish witch preparing for her bat mitzvah, and the forthcoming *Book of Candles,* a picture book for Hanukkah. Laurel's books have been awarded such honors as the Sydney Taylor Book Award and the Geisel medal, and she teaches in the MFAC program at Hamline University. Laurel's Passover secret is that she actually loves the taste of raw horseradish!

Chris Baron (he/him) is the award-winning author of novels for young readers including the verse novels *All of Me*, an NCTE Notable Book; *The Magical Imperfect*, a Sydney Taylor Notable Book and *School Library Journal* Best Book of 2021; *The Gray*; and *The Secret of the Dragon Gems*, a middle grade novel coauthored with Rajani LaRocca. He received his MFA in poetry at SDSU and is a professor of English at San Diego City College and the director of the Writing Center. He grew up in NYC and spent countless hours at Seders with his family in Long Island and now does his best to hold a Seder every year where everyone is welcome!

Adam Gidwitz (he/him) is the author of the Newbery Honoree *The Inquisitor's Tale* and the bestseller *A Tale Dark & Grimm* and its companions and of the bestselling series *The Unicorn Rescue Society*. He is also the creator and narrator of the podcast *Grimm, Grimmer, Grimmest*, so it is no surprise that telling the story of the Exodus as disgustingly as possible is his favorite Passover tradition.

———

Sofiya Pasternack (she/her) is a mental health professional, the highly distractible author of Jewish middle grade and young adult fantasy novels, and prone to oversharing gross medical stories. She's the author of *Anya and the Dragon*, *Anya and the Nightingale*, and *Black Bird, Blue Road*, which are all about Jewish kids kicking butt and are all Sydney Taylor Book Award Honors. Her favorite Passover tradition is making her cats act out scenes from *The Prince of Egypt* and also adding an orange to the Seder Plate.

———

Ruth Behar (she/her) was born in Havana, Cuba, and grew up in Queens, New York. She is a cultural anthropologist and an author who writes books for young people about immigration and searching for home. *Lucky Broken Girl* was inspired by the year she spent in a body cast, and *Letters from Cuba* was inspired by her grandmother's journey from Poland to Cuba to save her family on the eve of World War II. In her picture book, *Tía Fortuna's New Home*, she explores the suitcase of memories all immigrants carry. Her favorite Passover tradition is eating the Korech sandwich with Sephardic-style haroset.

Sarah Kapit (she/her) is the author of numerous books for middle grade readers. Her novel *Get a Grip, Vivy Cohen!* was selected as a Schneider Family Honor title and won the Washington State Book Award. *Second Chance Summer*, her most recent book, is a Junior Library Guild selection. Outside of writing, Sarah serves on the board of directors for the Autistic Self-Advocacy Network. She lives in Bellevue, Washington, with her partner and a goofy orange cat. Sarah's favorite parts of Passover include Chad Gadya and matzo balls.

A. J. Sass (he/they) is the critically acclaimed author of *Ana on the Edge*, *Ellen Outside the Lines* (a Sydney Taylor Honor Book), *Just Shy of Ordinary*, and *Camp QUILTBAG* (cowritten with Nicole Melleby). A. J.'s favorite part of Passover is attending various friends' Seder meals over the years and having the opportunity to meet new people. Originally from the Midwest, he currently lives in the San Francisco Bay Area with his husband.

Laura Shovan (she/her) is a novelist, educator, and Pushcart Prize–nominated poet. Her award-winning children's books include *The Last Fifth Grade of Emerson Elementary*, *Takedown*, and the Sydney Taylor Notable *A Place at the Table*, written with Saadia Faruqi. She is a longtime poet-in-the-schools for the Maryland State Arts Council and teaches for Vermont College of Fine Arts' MFA program in Writing for Children and Young Adults. Her latest poetry collection for kids is *Welcome to Monsterville,* illustrated by Michael Rothenberg. Just like Hannah in "Music and Matzo," Laura was the eldest cousin and only girl at family Seders!

Amy Ignatow (she/her) is the author and illustrator of *The Popularity Papers* and the Odds Trilogy and the author of *Jedi Academy: Christina Starspeeder Stories, The Cutest Thing Ever,* and *Symphony for a Broken Orchestra. The Popularity Papers* has been made into a live-action television series for YTV and STACKTV. Every year at Amy's seder a family friend insists on singing all fifteen verses of the Dayenu, and every year everyone else at the seder threatens to throw matzoh balls at him. Amy lives in Philadelphia with her family.

Veera Hiranandani (she/her) is an award-winning author for young people. Her most recent middle grade novel, *How to Find What You're Not Looking For,* received the 2022 Sydney Taylor Book Award and the 2022 Jane Addams Book Award and was a National Jewish Book Award finalist. Her novel *The Night Diary* won a Newbery Honor among several other awards, and her first novel, *The Whole Story of Half a Girl*, was a Sydney Taylor Notable Book. She's also the author of the Phoebe G. Green chapter book series and has many fond memories of finding the afikoman with her cousins growing up.